THE DEVIL YOU DON'T

A novel by

RON MOODY

Robson Books

FIRST PUBLISHED IN GREAT BRITAIN IN 1980 BY
ROBSON BOOKS LTD., 28 POLAND STREET,
LONDON W1V 3DB. COPYRIGHT © 1980 RON
MOODY.

*All the characters in this book are fictitious, and any resemblance
to actual persons, living or dead, is purely coincidental.*

British Library Cataloguing in Publication Data

Moody, Ron
    The devil you don't.
    I. Title
    829'.9'1F   PR6063.05/

    ISBN 0–86051–101–4

Printed and bound in Great Britain by
REDWOOD BURN LIMITED
Trowbridge & Esher

PART 1

'Eternal passion...eternal pain'

Chapter One

Hugo's continuing dialogues with himself were a source of great satisfaction to himself. He was a perfect listener. He knew when to stop speaking to himself and begin listening. He also knew when to stop listening to himself and begin speaking. Above all, he never lied to himself. Self-deception topped his list of *'Great Crimes Against The Emergent Intellect'*. And at those times when his reflexive discussions reached the level of Platonic Dialogue, he also learned from himself.

Nonetheless, as he pulled up at the traffic lights where Parkway branches into Albany Street, he automatically stopped speaking and looked in his rear mirror. One day, when he had been chuntering away at some traffic lights, he had become aware of a large taciturn police car on his offside, with two silent men in uniform in the front and two mutes in plain clothes in the back. It appeared that they had had him under observation for a whole minute. And he was breathalyzed within the next. His proven innocence did not deter them from following him along the road for many more minutes before they finally let him off the hook. And he had learnt his lesson.

But by the time he had turned into the Outer Circle of Regent's Park at six minutes to eleven on this fine spring morning, he was once more in full spate.

'Six minutes to eleven on this fine spring morning, and Jenny's coming home tonight!' he said, and celebrated on the accelerator of his Peugot 504 Family Estate. A voice on Capital Radio began a hard sell on cut-price vegetables and he switched off with a contemptuous click!

'Bloody idiots! Jesus! Thirty-eight *pee* per pound for tomatoes, twelve *pee* per piece for grapefruit, what a bloody daft way to measure a currency. . . . *pee*! PEEEEEE! What a degrading, hyper-inflationary undersell for the once proud Pound Sterling! What happened to good old Ten Bob, Half a Crown, a Shilling? Good solid *sterling* sounds, not *peeeeeee*! Yuk! Bloody awful petty paltry name for a penny! *Say* penny! Penny! Not PEEEEEEEEEEEE!'

It occurred to him that this would be a good time to laugh at himself – which he did – then he went silent as his independent suspension floated him along the Outer Circle beside the classic Nash Terraces, and he opened his ears to the sweet sounds soaring up from the trees and shrubs and hedgerows on his right. He felt as if he were flying, in sympathy with the chirruping and chirping and cooing and cawing, all the textures of birdsong from a thousand tiny throats.

'What a piece of work is bird, eh Hugo?'

'Probably the last of the great vertebrates to appear on earth, old boy!'

'A cynical theist might say the last of God's works before he stopped inventing genera on this failed planet, hm?'

'Or the last of God's clues to the secret of salvation, friend?'

'And the birds will inherit the earth, yeah, yeah!'

5

'Sing away, sing away, for Jenny's coming home today! Oh, my God, I miss you, Jenny!'

He thought of her slim body and the barely perceptible breasts and a wave of gentle lust surged through his viscera; it brought his foot down on the accelerator, jerked his mind out of its reverie and his other foot on to the brake.

'Four minutes to eleven, precisely,' he murmured, and pulled up behind three other cars parked opposite Cambridge Gate, just before the Outer Circle goes into Park Street East and Marylebone Road, the last oasis of free all-day parking amidst the voracious meter zones of Central London. He sat and waited, watching the three wise drivers ahead of him, dismounted and chatting at the curb; watching the lesser fools behind, arriving to join the queue. At eleven o'clock, parking was permitted, but by that time the Outer Circle was lined with free-loaders for a mile back. It was a delicate, precise manoeuvre that delighted him every morning: the timing of his arrival, the defeat of the meter maids, the twenty-minute brisk walk (or tube if it rained) to Houghton Street, where he was a lecturer in Social Anthropology at the London School of Economics and a very fine fellow indeed.

'Clever, Hugo, clever and neat! Sing on, my sparrows and chaffinches!' He cocked his ear and quoted Matthew Arnold:

'*Listen Eugenia –*
How thick the bursts come crowding through the leaves!
Again – thou hearest?
Eternal passion!
Eternal pain!'

Eternal pain! He leaned back and closed his eyes for a moment. Eternal pain – the pain in love! The pain that comes with love . . . those accursed concomitants . . . bitter

6

with sweet ... thorn with rose ... syphillis with sex ...
the wasp on a sunny afternoon, coasting in on a gentle
breeze ... to find your arm as you bask in the sun ... and
sting you! His academic training forced him briefly to the
converse, the love in pain, the life-giving cactus in the
desert, the dock leaf and the stinging nettle, nature's remed-
ies to nature's ills, but there was no comfort in it ... still
the injustice of spoiled bliss, the sting in the sun, the pain
in love, tormented him. His love for Jenny, so deep, so
complete that it was a source of pain and it shouldn't be.
Oh, God! If she should leave him ever!

'You are twenty-three years too young; when I am sixty,
you will be thirty-seven,' he had warned her. 'And you
will fall in love with a younger man and leave me.'

'I did not hear that, Huggy,' she had said. 'Think upon
the quality of life, you old fool! Ten years of happiness at
your geriatric side will be more than enough.'

If she should leave him ... could he never let the thought
escape? *The summer of '75* ... he lowered his head on to
the steering wheel. Up ahead, a car door slammed shut.

'Everybody out!' Number One smiled at him through
the windscreen and waved. Hugo climbed out, locked his
steering wheel and door, and set off in the bright sunshine
for Houghton Street. He liked the walk past Senate House
and the other colleges, linking them to LSE, endowing
that small village in Clare Market with the sense of University that one rarely felt outside Cambridge.

He thought briefly about where he would take Jenny
tonight if she wasn't too tired after the drive down from
Cumberland; and if he had any energy left after he had
welcomed her home with a giant helping of copulation,
et seq., inter alia, and all that animal jazz. His mind leapt
to Reisser.

'Undergraduate pig! Bloody know-all!' he muttered. He
had a tutorial at twelve, and he knew the bombastic little

7

bastard would have dug up something Hugo hadn't read, just to hammer the student-teacher relationship into a pointless free-for-all of quasi-equal minds. You never knew whether you had a genius on your hands or a brazen idiot until the buggers took finals and the big mouths swallowed a lower second and the worm in the corner crawled in with a first.

'I really don't like the little sods,' he said to the portico of the British Museum. 'Their propensity to learn is interred in the immensity of their ignorance.'

Hugo loved his epigrams; he also loved his work, his insight, his perception, his university, his academic status. He knew his craft – four years' fieldwork in the Congo had set the seal on his career – and he had written books to prove it!

'You are frozen-faced, implacable strangers to each other,' he observed of a queue of natives, waiting for communal transport in Kingsway, 'and I take great delight in reducing you to empirical terms of reference consistent with deductive schema, and filing you away in the pigeon-holes where you belong! So there!'

He reached Houghton Street just after eleven-twenty and nodded his way through the mob of students who traditionally spent more time on the steps than in the library. He waved to the porters who had been there when he was an undergraduate and had probably broken their nails hoisting up the foundation stone. He walked up the stairs because the lift was always crowded and slow and he enjoyed the challenge of making it in one to the fifth floor without losing all his breath.

There was a note on his desk. From Reisser. He had been inevitably detained and would like another appointment.

'*Inevitably* detained? *Unavoidably*, you klott! There's a slip of the Teutonic pen if you like! Probably got his jaw locked or choked on his jargon!' Then Hugo realised he

8

had no appointments all day. He could finish some notes on his new lecture course and leave early, ready for Jenny. Good old Reisser, he'd always liked that immigrant Kraut!

Hugo was working out a course on modern approaches to the measurement of social phenomena, selecting the latest ideas in the brain market before they had been assimilated into standard critical textbooks. The traditional anthropologists had been reviewed and discussed and encapsulated by so many commentators and methodologists that they were now safely lumped into schools and neo-schools and crypto-schools, bearing more labels than pots of jam. But once disposed they were never again studied in sufficient detail or with the same care. Stuck in a corner of the mind, 'Functionalist', 'Structuralist', Malinowski, Radcliffe-Brown, Lévi-Strauss – the name alone was enough for a ten-page rundown. And so much was lost. He wanted to open it all up again and make the kids think for themselves. So now he was concentrating on new, unlabelled jam-jars – Goffman, Trivett, Laing, all the new boys – hoping the contents might prove at the last to have a lasting flavour.

The phone rang. He picked up the receiver, half aware; listened; roared with joy!

'Jenny! Jenny, how are you? Where are you, are you home already?'

'No, Huggy, I'm still here.'

His heart thumped and he pressed the receiver tight against his ear.

'Still there? Up there – in Cumberland? When will you be home? It's eleven-thirty now, when are you leaving?'

'I'm staying on, darling, just a few days more. . . . I have to. . . . I can't explain now but the story is more than I'd hoped.'

'What story? Are they still roasting the robins on Filingdale Moor? Don't say it, I made a bad joke. Jenny, why

9

don't you come back today, go up again later? Where are you?'

'Dear Huggy, don't make it difficult, I have to stay.'

Don't make it difficult, he wanted to shout at her, *how do you bloody women do it? You pain us and blame us and leave us to cry!* He swallowed it all back.

'Hey, wait a minute. You still at the Cold Pike Hotel? Look, I'll take a few days off and come up and see you. I don't –'

'*No!*' The intensity in her voice winded him. 'No, dear old Huggy, no . . . it's . . . it's easier if I do it alone. . . . I'm all over the place.' She paused, but he couldn't speak. 'It won't be long. I do miss you, darling, I miss you so much.'

'I love you, Jenny.'

'I love you, Huggy – oh, Jesus, look at the time, I must go. I'll be home in a couple of days, I promise. 'Bye, darling.'

''Bye, Jenny.'

There was a pause, and her voice came back very small and tiny and little.

'Look after yourself, love.'

The receiver clicked in his ear and he sat there for a century of indescribable loneliness, his eyes closed, nothing but the empty, staccato burring at the other end. He found his fingers were locked in a grip of steel, prised them loose and replaced the receiver. He leaned back in the chair, staring at the desk, trying to collect his thoughts.

'You are Dr Hugo Brill, Ph.D., B.Sc.(Econ.), social anthropologist, rational thinker (brain highly developed), scientific analyst, sometime philosopher, mocker of emotional excess, scourge of the meter maids, what the hell are you doing, moping over a girl, pull yourself together, man!'

Pull yourself together. Jenny had stayed away before, chasing up some extravagance of social injustice or ecological imbalance. Away and away again. But this time . . . there was . . . something in the tone of her voice he didn't understand.

He lit a cigarette, puffed it once and crushed it in the ash-tray. How he hated the way Jenny did that; huge, broken fag-ends all over the place. Now he was doing it too. Hateful habit. Ugh!

'Wasteful, stupid habit!' he shouted at the ash-tray. 'Horrible, ugly, bent fag-ends all over the place! Why buy the bloody things!'

He couldn't sit there. He stood up suddenly, wandered to the armchair beside the bookcase, slumped into it, arms on the rests, head thrust forward, sitting like a stone block. His eyes roved wildly for a moment, caught a flash of bright green under a pile of papers on the bookcase. He pulled it out and looked at it, letting his mind wander over the meaning of it, the pain it was causing him, slapped it fiercely down on to the floor at his feet, then read it, long-sighted, without his glasses.

'The Windscale Enquiry. Report by the Hon. Mr Justice Parker. Presented to the Secretary of State for the Environment on 26 January, 1978. Volume I. Report and Annexes, 3–5. H.M.S.O., £3.75 net.'

He picked it up again with a grunt of effort, and thumbed through it absently.

'Introduction. On 1 March, 1977, British Nuclear Fuels, Ltd., submitted to Copeland Borough Council an application (BNFL 4) under Section 23 of the Town and Country Planning Act, 1971, for outline planning permission for a plant for reprocessing irradiated oxide nuclear fuels and support site services at their Windscale and Calder Works, Sellafield, Cumbria . . .'

Justice Parker had opened a public inquiry at the Civic

Hall, Whitehaven, Cumbria, on May 17, 1977, and it had closed on November 4, the one-hundreth day of the hearings. One hundred days of witnesses, observers, tests and objectors, measuring the risks of terrorist attack and radioactive pollution against the fail-safe precautions and the undoubted rewards of an expanding nuclear energy programme in a world starved and blackmailed out of its traditional sources.

The Report was released to the public in March, 1978, and the papers had a field-day. 'Nuclear Dustbin Plan'; 'A-bombs in the Dustbin'; 'Britain, the World's Dustbin!'; and a pretty dangerous dustbin at that! The crux of the media protest was that the new plant would reprocess, each year, 1200 tonnes of spent fuel, half from British nuclear power stations and half from abroad. By an undoubted miracle of science, the spent fuel would be reprocessed into plutonium which would be used as fuel for a fast reactor which would produce *even more plutonium* which could be separated off and used again! So all at once there had to be voices crying out against 'The Plutonium Economy', the dangers of a world awash with plutonium, plutonium returned under the terms of the BNFL contracts to the countries originating the nuclear waste. And when the largest of these was Japan, scarred with memories of Hiroshima and Nagasaki, it didn't seem the wisest thing in the world to give her the means to make atom bombs. What puzzled Hugo were the idiotic terms of the contract.

'My God,' he had said to Jenny, 'you don't give the Japs or anyone else *pure* plutonium! The Parker Report says it can be "fixed", that is, we send it back as irradiated fuel rods, too dangerous to steal and no use for bombs. Either that or no deal!'

He understood the Report because he had extended his peripheral knowledge in all directions; not content with potted explanations, he had gone, at some length, into

12

atomic theory and the structures of the various nuclear reactors. He had a similar informed flirtation with physiology, geology, archaeology, and the internal combustion engine. A maddening chap to argue with. To be in love with. To be married to.

Jenny had been assistant editor for four years on *Change!*, a New Left, Eco-freak monthly, produced by assorted graduates who had left university behind and kept their revolutionary fervour up front; a no-holds-barred broadsheet which specialised in crimes against the environment, taking sides for and against everything from doomed whales to macrobiotic food, naming names and bringing high blood pressure to high places.

At the age of ten, Jenny, a bedraggled and duffle-coated schoolgirl, was one of the sixty-thousand footsore marchers slogging all the way from the Atomic Weapons Research Establishment at Aldermaston to the CND rally in Trafalgar Square, her mother pushing baby John in a fold-up pram, her father playing guitar and singing songs of protest. Blooded on the Campaign for Nuclear Disarmament, bred on its 'Ban The Bomb' philosophy, Jenny had hated Aldermaston as she now hated Windscale, loved Canon Collins and Lord Soper as she now loved Amory Lovins and Ivan Illich. Now she was twenty-nine and with every passing year had reaffirmed her purpose. 'Ban The Bomb!' had become 'Ban The Nukes!' ... *Change!* gave banner headlines to the Friends of the Earth conservationists, quoted Tom Burke verbatim, reported his grim warning that all those now giving judgment on the new Windscale plant bore a profound responsibility to the world and future generations.

There was no other way for Jenny. Hugo said she made Jane Fonda and Vanessa Redgrave look like hospital almoners. To her, health physicists and fail-safe engineers were little boys with thumbs in dykes, she was adamant that the power unleashed in the atom was truly beyond the comprehension and control of the atomic scientists who juggled, half-blind, with existence itself.

She had thrown the Report across the room.

'He admits it, Huggy, there it is in black and white. Look! "There will be additional exposure to local inhabitants!" Then he says the risks appear to be so small, etcetera, etcetera . . . *appear* to be? My God, how many cases of sterility and leukaemia does "appear to be" appear to mean?'

'I would say it refers to the fact, my love, the *fact* that in twenty-two years of operation, the safety of the reactors and the protection of their personnel from radiation has been developed with considerable success; the *fact* that the discharge of radioactive waste has been accompanied by increasingly effective monitoring of the environment.'

'You surprise me, Hugo,' Jenny had said, beginning to pace up and down, 'I didn't think you were so naive. You know damned well, we have got to stop the nukes *now* and go for alternative energy systems – the sun and the wind and the water and the earth!'

'Earth would seem to imply coal,' said Hugo pleasantly, 'and I think there may appear to be some truth in this report of the Electrical Power Engineers' Association, that by the end of the century, for every twenty people killed by radioactive pollution from nuclear stations, five thousand may die from the poisonous compounds released at coal-fired stations.'

'Two blacks don't make a white!'

'And that doesn't include the three hundred deaths due to coal mining accidents.'

'You *know* that isn't the point, don't come that bloody impartial statistical crap with me. We are not talking about five thousand people, we are talking about *survival*!' And then, as if to add weight to her argument, 'You're my husband now and that makes you a human being and not a machine!'

A human being and not a machine. My God, if only he were a machine, freed from the pain of loving, the torment of doubt, the vile human disease of jealousy. She had gone off to Cumberland the next day, sworn to find some flaw in the bland assurances of Lord Justice Parker, vowed to smash the Windscale project even if it meant diving into the sea and bringing back one blistered, irradiated fish . . . not one 'assumed' suffering from lymphocystis, but one proved dying from radioactive pollution.

And she had been away two weeks and now she was staying away for a 'few more days' . . . and her voice had that note in it he didn't understand . . . and the hell of it was he didn't give a damn about the Parker Report, he didn't give a damn about Windscale and Calder Hall and Fast Breeder Reactors and Japanese Atom Bombs! The hell of it was, he didn't know who the hell she was *with*!

He sat there for a brief moment longer, then stood up decisively. He packed the Report and other relevant papers into his case, checked his desk, wrote a hurried note for the department secretary, and left the office and the building.

Damn it *all*, he was going to Cumberland, to the Cold Pike Hotel, to see his wife!

Chapter Two

Once he was on the motorway, Hugo felt better. He had taken a taxi to Regent's Park, driven home to Hampstead in twenty minutes flat, packed an overnight bag, left a note for the milkman, checked his tyres, water, oil and petrol at the nearest garage, and here he was on the M1, just after one o'clock, and the sun was shining in a clear blue sky.

He kept to the fast lane most of the time at a steady ninety, slowing to seventy for the occasional police car perched on its little hillock like a predatory falcon; giving way to half a dozen road-hungry Cortinas and one omniscient Rolls, floating past in a cloud of Partagas; he sat steadily at the wheel without fatigue or awareness of the journey. His thoughts turned over and over like an inexorable tape recorder, over and over with visions of Jenny and sounds of Jenny and the touch and the feel and the approach of Jenny, every mile bringing her nearer to him.

'Oh, my goodness, Dr Hugo Brill, what has happened to you?' he said to himself. 'You are full of sentimental bull! Clear your mind, boy, get a hold of yourself!'

But he knew Dr Hugo Brill had been left behind, Hugo Brill, Ph.D., had stayed there in the office, slipped away from him with all that cherished self-control, those theories of positive thinking, that serenely rational self; left him now slithering down a slope of insecurity and dread, an ordinary man, God help him, who didn't trust his wife!

He remembered the day they had met, the very instant that they had met: his first class for fresher students, Michaelmas Term, 1967. Eleven years ago. His brow furrowed, he shook his head.

'Eleven years?'

Jenny had come into the room, all dirndl skirt and crochet blouse, dangling a string bag full of new books, holding a large folder, pausing at the door, looking for a seat.

He had felt a sharp jolt inside him, a feeling almost of recognition of somebody he had known for a long time. He found himself staring at her lovely face, waiting as her huge dark eyes came slowly round – and locked into his. Locked, hard and fast. Penetrating and deep. It may have been only a second or two that they stood like this, but they were suddenly in total contact, every segment in his body matching a segment in hers, a force field holding them parallel, frontal, joined by inflexible fibres of vibration and energy. He realised later that in that instant, they were two halves made one.

Yet they never exchanged one personal word for that whole term. Until the last day, when he met her by sheer chance in High Holborn, on his way to Gamages to do some Xmas shopping. She was going too. They went together. They looked at everything. They bought nothing. They went to a pub and had a sandwich. They discussed her course. They discussed LSE. He silenced her protests and paid the bill. They walked to Chancery Lane Underground. She silenced his protests and bought the tickets. They laughed, parted at Tottenham Court Road, went their separate ways in separate trains, opened their separate newspapers and didn't read a word.

Hugo took a deep breath and blew it out as a long sigh. He switched on the radio.

'. . . *news headlines* . . . *Passengers, delayed by a holiday strike at Manchester's Ringway Airport, waited up to thirty hours for their flights to the sun. When they eventually arrived on the Spanish island of Majorca, they found that their hotels were overbooked* . . . *Six restaurant workers were herded by raiders into a freezer room at the Century Hotel in Oklahoma City yesterday, and shot through the head one by one. Police launched the biggest murder manhunt in Oklahoma's history. Managers are concerned how much money the raiders have snatched* . . . *A keeper in a safari park was fighting for his life last night after being attacked by a chimpanzee* . . .'

'Now for the bad news,' muttered Hugo, and stabbed the button. A flood of pseudo-American and heavy drumming poured out from the set; he stabbed again and hit the jackpot with some Chopin. It was three o'clock, and he was half-way to Kendal, just passing Newcastle-under-Lyme. Good timing. He treated himself to a half-hour stop at Keele services, enjoying the break, enjoying the bustling crowds emerging from the anonymity of their Buy-British Renaults and Datsuns and Volkswagons, revealing themselves as families with children and dogs, until this moment rivals in isolation on the Motorway. He even enjoyed the steak pie and chips, apple pie and custard, coffee and capsule cream, lingered briefly at the bookstall and returned to the road refreshed. He liked driving. He always found that his tensions evaporated, the simple technique of controlling his speed and direction and immediate destiny eased them away.

By five o'clock, he had turned off the M6 at Exit 36 for Kendal and Kirkby Lonsdale and was in the Lake District. The six miles to Kendal were dual carriageway cut into the carboniferous limestones fringing the National Park, heavy layers of strata exposed nakedly where the engineers had carved their route.

'Calcium carbonate, skeletal remains of marine organisms deposited under the sea in sedimentary layers,' droned Hugo, fringe geologist, 'three-quarters of the earth's surface now made up of sedimentary strata once beneath the sea.'

There was nowhere in the world that could make you so aware, in such a short time, in such a small space, of the insignificance of Man. Every kind of rock formation, igneous, sedimentary, metamorphic, would be here, abundantly visible to the informed eye. And for Hugo, the uninformed eye, the unheeding ear, were the burthen of the blind and the deaf, the travellers through life who see and hear nothing. For Hugo, to live without knowledge, without perception – without conception – was to be not alive at all. He had envied Jenny, coming up here without him, had wanted to be with her then, to explore, to discover together. And even now his growing excitement at the diminishing distance between them was enhanced by his love for this awesome, time-spanning, evocative scenery.

He skirted Kendal briefly, reached Windermere and took the lakeside route, unable to keep his eyes from the breathless lake to his left and the plateaux and ridges of Silurian rocks to his right. Boundary walls of slate and sandstone curved up the lower slopes, turning with the contours like minor Walls of China. Hugh Walpole had seen the stone walls 'running like live things about the fells'. Hugo wished he had said that.

At Ambleside he took a breath, stretched his legs, and had a drink at the Lakeside Hotel. It was five-thirty, the sun was still high in the sky and time was on his side. A young man with a black tie and a double-barrelled name proved to be the manager. Hugo asked him the quickest way to the Cold Pike Hotel in Seascale.

'Yes, sir. The quickest way is across the Wrynose and Hardknott passes, following the old Roman road. But at this time of day I wouldn't advise it.'

Hugo raised his eyebrows. 'Be there danger on the fells?'

'It's a very tricky single track road, sir, and you have to pull aside for cars coming in the opposite direction.'

'That's O.K.,' said Hugo, 'I have a very thin car.'

The manager smiled at last. 'Well, have a go, sir. But if there is any mist on the fells, it can be dangerous.' He indicated a map on the wall. 'The main road goes down to Broughton-in-Furness and up along the coast.'

'It's a lot longer,' said Hugo, fully aware that it would almost certainly be quicker. He smiled back. 'Thank you. If I don't survive, you'll know I took the wrong route.'

He knew he was going to try it the hard way. If he didn't, he wouldn't know what he had missed. And the hint of danger intrigued him. It suited the mood of this whole mad trip, added piquancy to the impulsive jaunt, the uncertainty of his reception.

He drove out of Ambleside, around the northern edge of Windermere, half inclined to stay on the main road after all. But when the moment of decision came, he turned off towards the fell route.

'Come on, Hugo old boy, if it's good enough for Hadrianus, it's good enough for you! Where's your spirit of adventure, let's have a bash! Forward, lads, to the land of crags and monsters, forward, St George, to fight the fiery dragon!'

Soon he was away from the area of habitation sprawled along a winding country lane, and out in a vast, open space of flat rock and marshland, enclosed by wire fences like a huge corral. He arrived at the bottom of a steeply ascending track, took a breath and passed on.

'AAARGH! Be this the dangerous pass?' he growled. It seemed easy enough; a car came towards him; they passed without pulling aside. He was rising all the time, gaining a point of view across the lowlands to his right. All around him giant outcrops of volcanic rock were set in a bed of dried brown fern and rough grass.

'Beautiful, oh, beautiful! How Jenny would love all this!'

Jenny. Jenny. Even here he could only think of Jenny. And the way it was. That Xmas had been without repose. He had realised that his feelings for this eighteen-year-old slip of a girl, this enchanting, capricious child, could get dangerously out of control. He had forced her from his mind, gone out a lot with all his sexiest, grown-up ladies, had a wild fling of parties, got lots of useless presents and one beautiful set of engravings. By New Year's Day, he had put his house and his mind in order. He had a heavy term ahead, and he dare not let himself be involved in any way with an egocentric teenager who would inevitably be having wild affairs with tall, athletic young students in no time at all. So in the Lent Term he was Dr Hugo Brill, forty-one years old, master of the lecture podium, distant but pleasant, smiling but aloof. Jenny was one of the kids in his class, a good student set realistically in her place, and Hugo was himself again.

Until one day, a solitary red rose appeared on the desk in his office. He put it in water. When it died, another appeared. His secretary had no idea where they came from. The rose term passed, and on the last day he went for a walk in Lincoln's Inn, to watch the tennis players in the spring sunshine. Jenny was there, looking far too beautiful and far too sure of herself – and carrying a single, solitary, red rose.

'I thought you'd need this to get you through the vacation,' she said.

Dr Hugo Brill grimaced to conceal his smile.

'Miss Lake, I do appreciate your good intentions, and my sombre study has benefited from your skills in floral design.' He wanted to take this stunning girl in his arms and tell her he would miss her like hell in the next few weeks. 'But perhaps an apple would be more appropriate . . . for a teacher.'

She put the rose in his hand. 'I'll miss you,' she said, and walked away.

The rose ended up pressed in Malinowski's *Magic, Science and Religion*.

By next term, Dr Hugo Brill, resplendent on the lecture podium in a new tweed suit and bow tie, was snatching covert glances round the New Theatre to catch sight of his Jenny, and presto! – once assured of her presence – a most diverting fellow! New bon mots sparked off his talk on 'Stigma'. Jenny roared with the rest. His tract on 'Marginal Man' took on some racist jokes to illustrate the acceptable face of prejudice. The students roared; Jenny sat unsmiling. Alone with her at her next tutorial, he could not resist comment.

'Well, Miss Lake, you do not appear to find my illustrations of racist jokes very funny. Laughing at prejudice is not prejudiced laughter.'

'But Dr Brill, racism is not a laughing matter. Satire can too easily feed its target instead of destroying it.'

'Very nicely put, if somewhat prosaic. I think we might have that in the form of a paper – without humour, of course – for our next class.'

Jenny got up and took the rose from its vase and threw

22

it in the waste-bin. 'The rose is dead,' she said, and for no apparent reason burst into tears.

'Miss Lake, no, no,' said Hugo, and stood up to put his arm around her. She turned at once, buried her face in his shoulder. 'Why are you crying, why are you upset? Hm?'

She turned her face up to him.

'I love you, didn't you know?'

'Yes,' said Hugo.

Jenny graduated in 1970 with an Upper Second in Sociology. She rushed up to his office and told him and he said if she hadn't messed so much with student politics she would have got a first. Then he kissed her.

She was twenty-one and Hugo was forty-four, and that was the day he asked her to marry him.

Hugo swerved violently to avoid a large rock on the road. A moment later, he coasted downhill, braked hard at a sharp bend where a small signpost said 'Wrynose Pass, 1 : 4', and he was into it. A single track, soaring to heaven, twisting and turning up and down in 1 : 4 gradients. His eyes were riveted to the road, his hands welded to the wheel, this wasn't dangerous, this was fun! The switchback took him out of everything but the sheer joy of driving, the steep, jagged flanks of Kettle Crag and Pike O'Blisco towering on his right, Blake Rigg and Wetherlam on his left. All the 'beauty, horror and immensity' that Dr John Brown had seen here two hundred years before. The descent into the Duddon Valley was almost an anticlimax. But he marvelled at the winding becks and gills cutting into the heavy turf, in narrow troughs sometimes only a foot wide and a foot deep.

'My God, becks and gills and tarns and fells and crags and pikes and hows and riggs – those Norsemen had a way with words, the names are bloody beautiful!'

Beautiful, and not without horror. For the valley sides were covered with a mass of tangled, dark green brush, like a mop of unruly hair; everything was askew, everything in this beautiful, incredible, wild, frightening place, tormented from its natural shape by the caprice and whim of nature. Until ten thousand years ago, the ice had been at work. It was really a place to be alone in; to be terrified of all that was dark and mysterious in a land of rocks and forests and bottomless lakes, where swimmers sank without trace. But, by heaven, he wasn't alone.

The slopes and sides of the tracks were swarming with fell walkers with heavy boots and strong sticks and bright cheeks. The cars before and behind him, pulling aside and passing, braking hard and changing down, were filled with human faces, all smiling graciously in their shared peril. And perilous it was, for suddenly he was past the Duddon Valley and rising again – it wasn't over yet, worse to come – now he was twisting and turning in 180-degree hairpin bends and 1 : 3 gradients, headed for the Hardknott Pass! The joyous mood of his surprise trip turned to a grim realisation that this really was quite dangerous! The proximity of the fell walkers and other cars did nothing to relieve the sheer blood-tingling terror of steering his agile little Peugeot Estate (thank God he had a skinny car!) along this narrow, tortured track between the massive crags of volcanic rock. 'Beauty, horror and immensity', yes, the overpowering majesty and danger of nature, changing, changing, through fire and water and ice for two hundred million years. His intellect was insignificant, his clever petrol-driven car was insignificant, the world around him never so immense.

He came to a steep rising bank – hell, it had to be forty-five degrees straight up! He slammed into bottom gear and dare not change lest his engine stall and he roll back into the car behind; the track turned even as it rose into vicious hairpin bends that kept every muscle in his body steel-taut. He began to think he couldn't hold the ascent, higher he

24

went and higher, was he at the top? Oh, Jesus, no! . . . Yes! the winding trail was taking him down, he was back on level ground stretching away into the distance. He pulled into the first convenient bay, and let his stomach come back into place.

It was six-thirty. If it didn't get any worse he should be in Seascale by seven o'clock. He sat and looked around and admired his own guts. Imagine going any other way!

'You did it, Hugo, you smug bastard!'

He looked back, gloating at the strained faces of the drivers arriving behind, rigid in their seats as they came back to earth. Then, with a small pang of disappointment, he realised he hadn't seen the Roman camp on the south-western slope of Hardknott; Mediobogdum, built on a grassy shelf commanding a view of the Esk Valley from the hills down to the sea. He mused on the Roman garrison cutting that grim route from Ambleside to Eskdale nearly two thousand years ago, warm-blooded Italians, posted from the blazing sunshine of the Mediterranean to this God-forsaken outpost. Not aloof, classical heroes, but sybaritic ancestors of every restaurant owner in Soho.

'Eh, eh, Mama!' Hugo grinned, waving his arms, 'wassamatter, what-a-for I come to this-a-stinking place, huh? S'nuff to give-a you da spooks, huh?'

He loved the Romans. So did Jenny. They had spent their honeymoon in Rome. Stayed at the Hotel de la Ville in the Via Sistina near the Hassler-Medici at the top of the Spanish Steps. It was the 'English Quarter' of Rome, the kind of place, said Jenny, they would have come to Rome to be away from if it had been even remotely English. Hugo alone knew what she meant. But the Spanish Steps had a magic of their own. In the evening they would stand on the upper terrace, side by side, hand in hand, absently aware of finger exploring finger, nail clicking on nail, tiny, small, intimate, caressing; aware of the sunken houses each

25

side, their stucco walls shading down from rich orange browns to pale, dusty fawns; aware of a thousand swifts, wheeling and swooping in the dusk, whirring above them in the air like stretched rubber bands.

Hugo had envied Keats's house at the foot of the Steps until Jenny reminded him that Keats had come here to die – within six weeks – a helpless invalid, seeking the sunshine to sustain his fading life.

They had breakfasted one morning in Babbington's Tea Rooms on the opposite corner, were horrified to find themselves actually having tea and crumpets in the middle of Rome. So they had most breakfasts on the marble-paved terrace outside their room, looking up at the green shuttered courtyard, flanked by endless pots of geraniums; these seemed to be the source of the tiny red spiders, swarming everywhere, barely visible and evidently carniverous, because small bites appeared on them and they never knew why. But breakfast sometimes didn't happen, with the 'Non Disturbate' notice outside the door, and Hugo and Jenny in bed, looking deep into each other's eyes, looking, searching, peering, until he knew every millimetre of her irises and pupils and lashes, every faint nuance of colour in her deep hazel, blue, brown, violet eyes ... lying there, exploring the depths of each other's heart and mind and soul ... and love. And so Rome, the Eternal City, had become their city, the eternal guardian of their memories of love and mutual discovery, their eternal flame, welding them together for ever and ever.

'Ever and ever! *Ever and ever?* Oh, come on down to earth you stupid, damned fool, there is no such bloody thing!'

He jerked his head round, stared up the side of the fells. Against the sky a dark shape circled and disappeared.

'A buzzard!' Hugo searched eagerly for another sight of it. 'A real buzzard, first time I've seen a buzzard! What are the old wives' tales on that? Oh, sod the old wives, let's get on!'

He switched on and drove back on to the road, filled with an anger he didn't care to comprehend. Maybe because it had always been there beneath the surface. The pain in love. The hell of caring too much. Well, at least the hell of driving was over; he came to the lower valley of the Esk, a broad plain where the river tumbled and frothed gaily, relieved as Hugo to have left the perilous heights. The danger and wonder of the journey were over and he was plodding along at a merely risky sixty, along the narrow winding lanes, stopping only for a wide school bus or a flock of sheep hogging the road in transit from field to field. He reached a main road sign-posted for Seascale or Egremont and turned left, with an awful, sinking feeling that he should never have come at all.

The Cold Pike Hotel was set back about one hundred yards from the coast, and ten yards from the local railway line. He noted with some relief that it was three-star, he hated pokey, over-personal guest houses. As he parked the Peugeot in front of a white-painted block that adjoined a huge building in old red sandstone, he found himself rehearsing lines. Affection? Mischief? A hint of forced flippancy? 'Look who's here then!' 'I had a couple of days off and here I am!' 'We – e – ll!'

The white portico led into a reception area that had a raised gallery with a wall lined in green slate. The reception desk to his right backed on to a wood-panelled stairway. Through glass doors he could see two bars, one each side. The receptionist, talking to a grey-haired old man, turned as he came in.

'Yes, sir?' she smiled.

'Ah, yes. You have a Mrs Jenny Brill staying here.'

The receptionist looked puzzled. 'No, sir.'

Hugo found himself unheeding and persistent.

'This is the Cold Pike Hotel?'

'Yes, sir.'

'Well, my wife, Mrs Jenny Brill, called me from here at eleven-thirty this morning and said she was staying on for a few more days.' The receptionist looked down at the register and nodded and Hugo took heart. 'She's been here for two weeks; Mrs Jenny Brill.'

'Yes, sir, I know her. Here, "J. Brill". She booked out at twelve o'clock this morning.'

Chapter Three

Hugo found himself staring at the receptionist for some moments, trying to find something to say, seeing it was quite useless to argue, the girl was quite definite. He heard himself, at last, murmuring something like 'Did she leave a message?' and heard the girl saying 'No, sir,' and he knew all the time there would be no message because Jenny didn't know he was coming. Then suddenly he had his wits back.

'Wait a minute, now, my wife called me from here at eleven-thirty this morning to say she was staying on; you say she booked out at twelve o'clock?'

'Yes, sir, I remember clearly. She paid the bill and left.'

'In a taxi?'

'No need, sir, I believe she took the train. She hired a car from Seascale Autos while she was here, paid by credit card. They collected it at one o'clock.'

Hugo made a mental note to check train times and the car hire company. He still wasn't satisfied.

'Look – she wouldn't call me and say she was staying on and then leave half an hour later.'

'Did she know you were coming, sir?'

Hugo lowered his head, not wanting to tell her; Jenny might have called him after he had left. He looked round, sighted a telephone booth by the entrance.

'No. Can I use that 'phone?'

'Of course, sir.'

He dialled Operator and put in a collect call to London. He listened to sixteen burrs at the other end and hung up. She wasn't home yet. If she had gone home. He thought about calling the offices of *Change!* in High Holborn, but it was already seven-fifteen and they worked office hours. That always amused him, a revolutionary magazine, changing the world between nine and five-thirty. He looked at his watch again; seven-fifteen, and he didn't quite relish another dose of 'beauty, danger and immensity' or even the coastal route back. And, besides that, he had a strong feeling that Jenny was still up here. She was here, somewhere! He was breathing heavily and his heart was thumping. Somewhere! With whom? He went back to the desk.

'Which room was my wife in?'

The girl looked at the register. 'Er – 27, sir.'

'Did she leave anything behind?'

'No, sir, she took her case with her.'

'So the room is quite vacant?'

'Yes, sir.'

'Well, I'll take it for tonight. It's too late to drive back.'

For a moment he thought the girl hesitated, almost as if she had been caught out, seemed about to ask someone if she was allowed to let him have it. Hugo found himself looking round at the old man; he was reading a paper. The girl smiled.

'Of course, sir. Will you please sign here?'

He filled in the booking form, took the key and picked

up his bag and briefcase. No porters? Three-star? Huh!

Room 27 was up the small flight of wooden, balustraded stairs that lay behind the reception desk, and along a winding corridor.

He opened the door with a sudden hope that she would be waiting for him, would spring out, yelling 'Surprise, surprise, Huggy, had you worried there, didn't I?' But the room was empty.

He dumped his bag and briefcase in the middle of the floor and sat down on a small armchair, noting the worn brocade and the chipped paint on the legs and not really caring. There were two beds in the room, an incongruously modern basin in the corner, and a window overlooking the sea front. The walls were off-white paper, peeling with damp near the cornice; the carpet was abstract kitsch, with more browns and yellows and greens than the Cumberland fells – why the hell was he looking at all this boring bloody trivia in such infuriating detail, why wasn't she *here*, waiting for him, waiting to drag him beneath that dingy coverlet to make instant, adoring love? Was she, God save him, making love to somebody else – somewhere else not far away? His stomach ached with a kind of grief, his heart fibrillated and thumped. He was shaking, shivering and he wasn't cold. Then suddenly he thrust himself out of the chair and strode to the window.

'Oh, Hugo, you poor, fifty-two-year-old, self-pitying creep, crawl out of your miserable navel and pull yourself together! It may be all in your paranoid mind! She may be home now, wondering who *you* are with! And if she's with someone else, he's only got her body, not her mind, and so what! So what, it's happened before!'

Happened before. Happened before! Yes, it had happened before. Face it, Hugo, bring it out, put it up front and look at it, bring it into focus, fight it, drive the canker out of your heart and soul, remember who you are, Dr Hugo Brill, B.Sc., Ph.D. . . .

31

It had happened before in the summer of '75, when Hugo and Jenny had been married for five wonderful years and she had been assistant editor of *Change!* for one whole year of red-hot words and banner headlines; the summer when she had gone off for a week to a conference of radical journalists in Newcastle and a letter had arrived, telling him she was staying on for a few days to tie up some loose ends; the summer when a terse 'phone call told him she had got herself involved with a macrobiotic guru and she needed to stay up there to think it out.

It had been a ravishing Sunday afternoon, and he had put the 'phone down and looked out of the window at the clear blue sky, with white tufts of cloud, and birds wheeling and singing, and the fragrance of flowers and the beauty of it all ... and the image of Jenny and her guru, strolling hand in hand. Where? Along Hadrian's Wall, by Housesteads Fort, looking out over the rolling Northumberland plains, hand in hand? Alnwick Castle, the green sward sloping up from the river to the battlements, hand in hand? Crossing a stile, a moment of intimacy, a look, brushing, touching, hand in hand? *My God!* He had felt such a desolate loneliness that day, such a bitter hatred for them both. The thought of another man touching her, even a tender glance exchanged, taking one mote of her total love for him, was too much to bear. He wanted them both dead! He had an impulse to smash everything that was hers, tear up all her letters, papers, photographs, throw her clothes out into the street!

In the end, he had walked out of the house, walked and walked and looked at the world without seeing a damned thing, trying in vain to blank out the pain, to dampen the fire in his soul to a tolerable flicker.

After two days, she had come back. Nothing had happened, she'd said, it had been a time for reassessment, a spiritual rebirth, a walk in the wild wind, a return to the home where Hugo lived. They never spoke of it again. But it had happened. *Happened!* And from that time on, Hugo had never been sure it wouldn't happen again.

'*Eternal passion . . . eternal pain.*' And the pain had never left him.

He picked up his suitcase, dumped it on the bed and opened the wardrobe. A musty smell exuded. 'I'll bet she liked that,' he mused. He left the door open, unpacked his suit and hung it up, took out his shaver and toothbrush, and noticed there was no telephone in the room, only some kind of intercom system over the bed. He should be calling home again, not unpacking. He would call in a minute, find she was there and have to pack and excuse himself to the receptionist like some bloody idiot and drive straight home. But no, he knew he was staying, he knew she wasn't home or even on the way; he knew she had moved from here but was still somewhere around.

He went into the bathroom and noted it was pleasantly clean and reasonably appointed, but with no shower fitting or curtain. So typical of English Parochial, he thought. Then he stopped, and stared at the soap rack across the bath.

Odd! How odd! There was a small piece of hotel soap, barely used, in the chrome basket. But Jenny didn't leave soap. It was one of her little caprices, one of his dear girl's peccadilloes – she always took the pieces of soap from hotels and added them to a multi-coloured, many-odoured soap mountain which she had constructed in the bathroom at home. Why hadn't she taken this one? In a hurry packing? Distracted? How odd! He went back to the bedroom, preoccupied, picked up the briefcase and opened it. Inside, the bright green cover of the Windscale Report jogged his memory.

'That's what Jenny came to see, little Miss David, pitting her wits against Goliath.'

'Marvellous courage, that girl!'

'I'm not going to lose her, I'm not going to lose her, Brill, by Harry and St George, I'm not! But where is she?'

'At the plant? She wouldn't be there now, surely. You could ask ... they may know something ... they must know if she's been there!'

'Good thinking, Brill!'

He looked out of the window at the sun still above the horizon; it was seven-thirty and he couldn't stay here brooding for a minute longer. He snapped his case shut, placed it carefully on the bed, lined it up with the woven squares on the coverlet.

'Hugo, you mad, neurotic fool, hyperaesthesia will get you nowhere! Come on, move!'

He left it there, precise and neat, knowing it was a symptom of anxiety neurosis and rather pleased that he knew, at least, what he'd got; put the room key in his pocket and went straight out of the hotel. He had no idea how he was going, was in no mood to spend one second consulting road maps.

He just knew he had to head for Calder Bridge, north of Seascale, and drove off the way he had come. He followed the winding road under the railway bridge, barely realising he was choosing the two sides of a triangle, but the distances were too short to matter. He by-passed Drigg and met the A595 at Holmrook, headed for Gosforth. It was pleasant countryside, the houses and walls all built in blocks of the new red sandstone that lay along the coastal strip from Morecambe Bay to St Bees.

Then, as he passed Gosforth, heading for Calder Bridge, he saw it. He realised that he had, in fact, been seeing it for some time, not known what to look for. Huge, grey plumes of smoke, tinged with pink from the setting sun, were rising up ahead of him on his left. His spine tingled with apprehension at being even this near to a nuclear reactor;

34

he sensed the image of annihilation that sat, mushroom-shaped, in men's minds, linked names like 'Windscale' and 'Aldermaston' with 'Hiroshima' and 'Nagasaki' as chapters in a Doomsday Book that might, one day, take grim stock of the nuclear age. It was a strange sensation, travelling in a kind of diminishing arc around the rising plumes, seeming to stay in one spot, yet coming nearer every second. At Calder Bridge, he crossed the Calder River which entered the sea through Windscale, then he headed west along a small winding lane for about two miles.

The plumes grew larger by the minute and suddenly, into view, came two giant chimney stacks, gallery-shaped at the top, like lighthouses thrusting up at the sky. The plumes acquired plinths that resolved into enormous cooling towers, and he could now see that only three of the four towers were belching smoke. He was there!

The road branched left and right at a high wire fence that surrounded the compound, with 'Guard Dog' notices displayed prominently at intervals. Hugo found that he actually had a sensation of fear, a feeling that he was being watched, suspected for being this close. He took the left fork, and saw through the fence that the giant chimneys arose from two massive buildings about one hundred yards apart; that, straight ahead, he was approaching a main entrance gate fronted, with unexpected innocence, by an ordinary bus stop. A security guard in uniform, with a peaked cap, stood by a small brick building beside the gate. Hugo pulled up well away on the road and sat looking for a moment or two.

The size of the works was awesome. He had seen the photos and looked briefly at the scale drawing attached to the Parker Report, but he had not expected a plant the size of a small village, stretching beyond his view to the south and north. The huge cooling towers were in pairs, like chunky guards, stationed at each end of six massive buildings that sprouted pipes and staircases and steam from every corner.

He was suddenly aware that the security guard was watching him. He was equally aware that he was on an open public road, looking at a permitted public view. But he was also very aware that he had an irresistible urge to turn on his tail and scoot away before the balloon went up, before the armoured cars appeared and took him inside for questioning.

'Be calm, Hugo, this is Britain, that sort of thing doesn't happen here!'

'Yes, Brill, but somehow this isn't the time to ask daft questions about a missing wife! Especially when she might be waiting at home!'

'Quite right, Hugo, I think we'll check first and come back tomorrow!'

'Yes, Olly.'

He turned on his tail and headed, rather fast, in the opposite direction. But he didn't turn off to Calder Bridge, it was all too fascinating and scary to leave at once, he wanted to follow the wire fence round and study the monster from all angles. A huge, silver sphere rose up on his left, Jesus, it was like a sci-fi film, uncanny shapes of buildings, twisting gantries, infernal pipes leading every-where, but everywhere! He passed another entrance, saw more guards, looked straight ahead and kept on going. Maybe the first lot were buzzing the second lot to tell them there was a suspicious-looking Peugeot lurking at the perimeter.

'A foreign car, eh Roach?'

'Yes, sergeant.'

'Bring him in!'

'Yes, sergeant.'

'Roach!'

'Sergeant?'

'Dead or alive!'

Hugo laughed at his own joke and braked sharply. There was no more road! Only a very small entrance to Sellafield Station. This was it – the rest of the perimeter was the coast of Cumbria, beyond that the Irish Sea and the suspect fish, absorbing generous doses of caesium-134 and 137 from the Windscale pipelines, exposing local fish-eaters to as much as forty-four percent of the safety limit. Fish-and-chip eaters, walking round with all that radiation in their stomachs and knowing it was forty-four percent safe. Nice, but not too encouraging for the salt and vinegar.

Stopped for a moment, he was aware for the first time of the shrill cries of the herring gulls along the shoreline. Gulls eat fish, how much radiation can a gull absorb? He thought of that solitary buzzard over the Hardknott Pass, remembered the outcry in the early 'sixties when high concentrations of pesticide residues were found in the tissues of dead peregrines and ravens and buzzards, found in their eggs that failed to hatch. A ban was placed on the most toxic of the pesticides used in farming, and there was a slow recovery. The Lakeland birds were less affected than those in the rest of the country, probably because there was less opportunity in the Lake District for man to become too ingenious for his own, and everything else's, good. Nature and ice had kept him out. But for all his past bio-chemical blunders and genocidal gambles, here he was at Windscale about to launch an expanding programme of nuclear activity and admitting 'additional risk of exposure to local inhabitants' in a publicly-debated report!

Being this close to the source, sensing the awful power, the incredible energy that was being created in insidious silence so very near to him, he understood why Jenny could find no peace in inaction. Perhaps it *was* all safe. But – and oh, what a but – it might not be! Only this time it wasn't a case of pesticides and dead eggs, it was all life at stake. Jenny hadn't gone home! She hadn't given this place up! She was about here somewhere and he was going to find her.

He turned and headed back to the hotel, managing at every turn of the road to watch the plumes of smoke drifting up to the heavens, still tinged with pink, dominating the skyline, the earth, the lives of all those upon it. He switched on the radio to feel some contact with his fellows, hear a human voice. The news was on again.

'*A British soldier was gunned down and killed outside a church in Londonderry yesterday, only minutes after his wedding. Three masked terrorists opened fire. . . .*'

Hugo switched off and drove in silence for a moment. It was nearly dark now.

'Whichever way you turn, my friend,' he murmured, 'you meet the devil you know or the devil you don't.' He paraphrased Socrates. 'Which of them is the better thing, nobody knows but God.'

Chapter Four

The Cold Pike Hotel shone like a full three-star beacon in the darkness, welcoming lonely travellers; inside, it was cheerful and warm, bustling with life, the public bar packed with smiling faces, the reception hall transformed, having sprouted a thick-set young man in a dress suit who shuttled in and out, taking orders for dinner. Hugo booked a table for nine-fifteen and made a perfunctory check on the Hampstead number. Sixteen burrs, no answer; he clicked off, quelled the sinking feeling in his stomach and went upstairs.

He threw his coat over the chair, ran a bath and checked his shaver on the wall fitting. It worked. He shaved quickly, he had nobody to impress, just wanted to feel clean. He tapped out the loose whiskers into the sink, wondering, as he always did, how much shaved-off hair he would have collected in forty years if he had kept it all in a bag. He turned off the bath, contemplated its inviting warmth, and went back to the bedroom for his dressing-gown and slippers.

His briefcase had been moved! It wasn't lined up with the squares on the coverlet! It was about half an inch off line at one end. Minimal, barely noticeable to anyone who didn't have hyperaesthesia, an excessive attention to detail and order, brought on by anxiety and possibly a superstitious urge, even in a rationalist, to control tomorrow by appeasing the God of Husbandry today. Hugo not only had it, he knew he had it, and he knew he had put that case exactly on the line and it wasn't now! He opened it. Nothing had been touched. The Windscale Report lay on top, and he picked it up, recalling the shock of the visit, the silence, the meaning. He took the twenty-five inch map of the Windscale and Calder Works from the pocket on the back cover and, still meditating, took it with him into the bathroom.

'It can't be much of a high security risk if anyone can buy a detailed layout of the whole damned leviathan for a measly £3.75 net, now can it?'

He perched it against the wall, the folds kept it upright; he hung his clothes on the chair and very slowly lowered himself into the luxurious excess of boiling bathwater. At last, he was stretched full length, his head on the rim, his eyes closed.

'What a day this has been,' he murmured, 'what a dumb, mad journey, 275 miles, and here I am, stewing in a lobster pot in the middle of nowhere! My wife is missing, the receptionist was shifty, my briefcase has been moved. . . .' His eyes opened minutely; the sliver of soap was still there. 'And she didn't take the soap! And how, dear Hugo, are you going to wash yourself with that?'

He closed his eyes again. Minutiae that meant nothing, the briefcase, the soap, the receptionist's hesitation. Like being in a haunted house, everything takes on meaning and nobody gets any sleep. He squinted sideways at the map. That was behind it all. He'd been spooked by the

40

Windscale Witch! He looked at it, playing brain games, making lazy calculations. On a twenty-five inch map that new processing plant would cover at least six acres. The Calder Hall buildings were half an acre each. And those buildings under the lighthouses – about an acre each! Big stuff!

Enough of this, he had boiled enough, soaked the journey out of his limbs. He lathered himself surprisingly well with the sliver of soap, taking added satisfaction from the knowledge that it had been on intimate terms with Jenny, rinsed himself with running water, and dried off.

He dressed, putting on a clean shirt and pausing only to line his briefcase up with the coverlet again. ('Haha, this time I'll trap the dissembling swine, they will suspect nothing! Nothing!') he went down to dinner.

A very pretty waitress took his mind off everything. ('Beautiful eyes, why do they look at me like that? I shall tip her hugely!') But she didn't come over, the restaurant manager took his order. He saw there was halibut on the menu, but didn't fancy even one percent of caesium-134 in his stomach, so he ordered steak. Well, what's a little pesticidal residue here and there – he didn't lay eggs!

He looked around the restaurant. About a dozen tables occupied. Must be a wild night out for the locals. The men wearing suits and ties, the ladies dressed in the height of something, cigarettes thrust at right angles to their fingers, blowing smoke in their partner's faces, playing Bette Davis in *Now Voyager*. Hugo drank half a bottle of claret and by the end of the meal, the world was a better place.

The manager approached. 'Would you like a brandy, sir, a liqueur?'

'Ja, Herr Ober, I will have a cognac. Excellent food. I'm sure my wife dined here every night. Young woman, twenty-nine years old – er – brunette, hazel eyes, small mole above navel – er – Mrs Brill.'

'Oh, *yes*, sir, Mrs Brill. She did, sir. Dined in every night. Sat at that table, always reading papers and books.'

'That's her.' Hugo had to put it carefully, avoid sounding like a suspicious husband. 'Didn't she eat with her colleagues? She's a journalist, they always travel in packs.'

'Well, they weren't staying here, sir. Mrs Brill ate alone every evening.'

Hugo enjoyed the brandy immensely. So Jenny didn't have anyone with her. He had coffee, and as he was leaving, tipped the manager. Far too much. Forget the waitress's eyes, she'd only served the chips.

'Oh, thank you, sir. And please apologise to Mrs Brill, I didn't say goodbye to her. I saw her go out at twelve o'clock, but didn't realise she was leaving.'

'But she had her suitcase with her. Didn't she?'

'No, sir, I'm sure she didn't. She had a British Airways bag. No suitcase. Unless it was already outside.'

'Thanks. Goodnight.'

Hugo's mind was whirring. Minutiae, minutiae, methodological processes at work, too many years of perception, analysis, postulation, thesis, test, conclusion, theory proven, disproven, try again, minutiae, minutiae. . . .

He went into the bar and ordered another brandy. The barmaid was slim, blonde and chatty; a marked accent brought him slowly back into focus.

'Swedish?' Hugo raised his eyebrows. She nodded. 'You're a long way from home. What are you doing in this neck of the woods?'

'I married a man from Cumberland. I like it here.'

'Of course,' said Hugo, realising he had been patronising. He looked around the packed bar. 'Any of these people work at Windscale?'

'Most of them. My husband does. The plant provides a lot of work.'

'Yes. My wife was working up here for two weeks. She's

a journalist. Writing an article on the Parker Report.'

'The dark-haired girl? Mrs Brill? The one we called Joan of Arc? Hey, that was your wife? Then you're Professor Brill!'

'Dr Brill,' said Hugo. So Jenny had been dropping names again.

'How come you're here and she's not?'

'I drove up today to surprise her, and she'd already left.'

The blonde laughed. 'So the joke's on you, Prof.'

She saw his eyes and stopped, seemed about to say something and was called away. 'Coming, sir!' She moved along to serve on the adjoining counter.

'I thought I recognised your face! Haven't I seen you on television?' The voice came from a bar seat a few feet from Hugo. He turned and saw a man in his mid-fifties wearing a beautifully-made suit in small Prince of Wales check. He had a David Niven moustache and a voice to match.

'Weren't you on a programme about soccer violence, old boy, something like that?'

'Yes,' said Hugo, dreading the clichés that were coming his way. The BBC had asked him to chair a seminar on soccer violence last November; for weeks after he had been buttonholed on every street corner.

'Well, I agreed with most of the things you said and I don't do that very often. Agree, I mean. What was it now? You don't believe in fines or prison, but in social work.'

'No,' said Hugo, sinking his brandy, ready to leave, 'I recommended a socially useful deterrent. Warn the louts once, next time call them up in the army.'

'Save the taxpayer's money and clean up the terraces, yes, damned good idea! Can I buy you a drink, old boy?'

Hugo was about to decline, then remembered the room upstairs and decided he'd stay with the bright lights a little longer.

'Thank you. Brandy, please.'

'Two Remy Martin, dear!' David Niven knew his cognac. 'Large ones!'

The Swede brought them across and leaned over the bar to Hugo. Her eyes were large and blue and sympathetic; he felt she knew something and didn't know how to say it.

'Well, Dr Brill, you have a very lovely lady. But I told her – she shouldn't take things so seriously.'

'I can well imagine,' said Hugo. Jenny wouldn't have missed any of this. Workers from Windscale, slaves from Lang's *Metropolis*; she had probably probed them all with a Geiger counter.

'Did Mrs Brill say anything about – ?'

'Mrs Brill! I remember her!' said Check Suit. 'Very beautiful gel. Very! Nearly started a riot here last week. Wanted the whole damn plant shut down! Haha! Bless her, she was marvellous!'

'She sure got guts,' smiled the blonde then shook her head. 'But why does she have to be so –' She screwed her eyes up, looking for the word. 'Bitter? A sweet kid like that?'

'She believes somebody has to do something, and with all the apathy around her she has to go at it that much harder.'

'Yes, but look where it leads to,' said Check Suit. 'I read an article that said today's terrorism in Europe is rooted in the student unrest of the 'sixties. Why? Nice, middle-class kids, well brought up, everything they want – so they want to kill and maim and blow everybody up!'

Hugo nodded. In Britain it had led to the relatively amateurish Angry Brigade. In Germany it had spawned the Baader-Meinhof gang, ruthless anarchists and killers.

'I mean, all this Red Brigade stuff in Italy, shootin' knee-caps, murdering public servants, it's all madness! How do your theories explain that, Dr Brill?'

Hugo sat a moment, thinking of Rome, thinking of

Jenny, the Spanish Steps, Keats and Shelley . . . now with more terrorist attacks per square kneecap than anywhere in the world. He sighed deeply.

'The Red Brigade is widely based, it has attracted working-class support, they feel the Communists, with their rigid dialectic approach, have sold them out. But I suppose the answer to your question is, it's in the nature of the beast.' Check Suit and the Swede (Hugo never got people's names) were hanging on his words, looked perplexed. 'What I mean is, man is the only species that kills its own – for pleasure! That, and a progressive deterioration in the quality of war.'

'Now you have me,' said Check Suit. 'I don't follow.'

'Well, briefly, in the Age of Chivalry, knights engaged in hand-to-hand combat on a chosen field of battle, honoured a defeated enemy, treated war as a sport. In the fight against Hitler, we progressed to the concept of Total War, no quarter given, no humanity expected, victory at any price.'

'Well, we had to beat the Hun,' said Check Suit.

'Of course.' Hugo knew he was wasting his time. He could imagine Jenny trying to reach these people, coming up against the impenetrable wall of the closed mind, the no longer teachable child.

'Today,' he persisted, 'today we have the gangs of terrorists who have effectively declared war on society, consider themselves ideologically justified in beating their equivalent of the Hun. For them, a world at peace has no meaning. I suppose we can blame the jolly idea on Che Guevara and his urban guerrillas. No formal declarations of war, no meetings of armies, no battlefields to be hallowed on regimental banners, just dirty, ruthless, back-street murders and to hell with who gets killed.'

'Ought to shoot the lot of them,' said the Swede.

'Yes! They would understand that! They would welcome the recognition that the war is on. But terrorism is treated as a peace-time policing operation; catch them and put them in prison. So they take hostages, get each other out, the undeclared war proliferates!' Hugo smiled. 'The only ones who understand it, recognise it, are the Israelis, who have been on a war footing ever since the foundation of their State.'

'And they're going to drag us in,' muttered Check Suit.

'No,' said Hugo. 'Nobody is going to be dragged into an open conflict, world war. That's the huge joke. They are all, still, much too afraid of the Bomb!' There was silence for a moment, then the hubbub around them rose up to remind them where they were. 'The ultimate deterrent, old Adam, ticking over a few miles away, churning out nice, peaceful megawatts of electricity. And for that we should thank God!'

Hugo stopped. He had been drawn out too much, wanted to change the subject.

'Incidentally, I'd like to see it,' he said. 'Windscale. Is it possible to get inside?' They looked at him. 'Silly to be so near to a modern miracle and not take the opportunity to look round.' He felt that tingle again. As if this were a war-time bar, with 'Careless Talk Costs Lives' all over the wall, and Hugo, a Nazi spy.

'Oh, they do have visitors, university students, accredited journalists. But I think they need to know who you are.' Check Suit chuckled. 'No problem, of course, for a university don, eh?'

The Swede put her hand on Hugo's arm. 'Tell you what, Prof. The boss knows 'em up there, I'll ask him what he can do.'

She wiggled through a side door leading to the reception. Check Suit leaned closer, confidentially. 'I'm in real estate, old boy. And I tell you, if they stop arguing and build the new plant, it will do us all a bit of good. More employment,

46

more housing, bonanza! Atomic dustbin? Pah! Newspapers get a touch hysterical don't you think?'

'I don't know,' said Hugo, 'I really don't know.' He had the feeling he was being quizzed again. And after that hair-raising drive around Windscale, he wasn't sure what he did think. The brandy was getting through, taking the bitterness out of the day. It would all come right in the morning.

The barmaid came back and held his arm again.

'Can't do anything about it now, but he'll let you know first thing tomorrow.'

'You are very kind,' smiled Hugo, and turned to Check Suit. 'Another – old boy?' Check Suit raised his arms to heaven in supplication. 'And you – what will you have, Miss Sweden?'

'Gin and tonic, darling.' She was a nice girl. David Niven was nice. Everyone was nice. Why wasn't Jenny here, making it nicer still? Maybe the barmaid knew.

'Tell me, did Mrs Brill say anything when she was leaving? Where she was going? Anything?'

'That's what's really strange,' said the barmaid, sipping her drink and putting it under the counter, making up her mind. 'She came in for a quick Guinness at lunch time and said she'd see me later. She didn't say she was leaving or anything.'

'Didn't she have her suitcase?' Hugo said, frowning.

'No, just a British Airways bag on her shoulder.'

'Correction, old gel!' Check Suit turned a slightly pink eye towards them. 'I came in for the usual at twelve o'clock and met her outside the front door. She did have her suitcase and she bid me –' He winked at Hugo. 'Bid me a fond farewell! You know what?' He roared with laughter. 'She's run out on you, old lad, that's what!'

Damn you, David Niven, thought Hugo, I wanted . . . then he wasn't sure what he did want. Surely it was better

47

if she had booked out ... or was it? He couldn't think straight. He'd had enough of the whole damn thing. He drank the brandy down, put his hand lightly on Check Suit's shoulder, fond wave to Miss Sweden, mustn't stagger, walk carefully to the door, up those horrendous, creaking stairs, what was it, Room 27?

The briefcase was exactly as he left it – well, of course it bloody was! He got to bed as fast as he could and lay there a while, wishing his viscera would stop swimming up and down inside him. He lay, wide awake, the moonlight streaming through the window, the distant surf washing the shore away in the distance. He just wasn't sure what he wanted. Too many signposts, pointing in too many opposite directions.

Minutiae, minutiae ... the receptionist had hesitated ... Jenny hadn't taken the soap ... the restaurant manager hadn't seen her suitcase ... the Swede hadn't seen the suitcase ... Check Suit *had* seen the suitcase ... couldn't think straight ... wait a minute ... either she did book out, suitcase and all, at twelve o'clock ... gone home ... gone away with another guru ... hell! Or what ... what was the other ... thing ... or Jenny had not checked out ... Check Suit was mistaken ... lying? ... and her bag ... without the sliver of soap ... had been packed ... by somebody else ... after she had left. ...

Chapter Five

An alarm bell went off in his ear and jerked him out of a deep sleep! Heavy sleep, heavy head, heavy as lead, queasy stomach, damn the drink! Sleep? Did he sleep after all? It had been a ghastly night. No, he couldn't have had a wink of sleep, not one moment of blessed unconsciousness, only a stream of words whooping through his head on a roller-coaster of unfinished sentences. Words, words, words, rolling up into the light of awareness and disappearing again before they could resolve into meaning. The alarm shattered him again! Jesus, it wasn't an alarm, it was the intercom. He winched up a heavy arm, pressed one of the buttons and hoped for the best. A voice told him that the hotel manager had fixed it. If he could be at Windscale Main Gate by nine-forty-five, he would be shown round. It was eighty-thirty!

He was out of the bed and into the bath – the wafer of soap gave of its last – shaved and dressed; snatched a quick breakfast, actually served in the room, went downstairs, told the receptionist he was staying on – same girl,

not the least bit shifty by day – and was out of the hotel by
nine-ten. No time to brood any more, it was time for
action! He didn't even call home, in case nobody answered.
He was in no mood for that. If she was back home, he was
acting like an idiot. On the other hand he was up here anyway, and he was going to see the Windscale demon at first
hand and by daylight. Everyone should see it, make up
his own mind. So nothing was wasted.

The plumes were still up in the sky, four today, guiding
him like Indian signals across the prairie to Fort Windscale.

'Doggone it, Marshall,' Hugo snarled, 'Ah guess it
ain't safe for man nor beast. But ah'm a-goin' in thar an'
ain't nobody gonna stop me! Nope!'

'Ah wouldn't do thet if ah was you, Brill!'

'Smile when y'say thet, Marshall. Yip!'

It was a beautiful morning and Hugo was in high spirits.
His pragmatic mind warned him that he was going to be
shown a very ordinary power station, with very ordinary
generators and pipes and cooling towers. Except this one
ate atoms, not coal or oil. Mankind takes giant steps then
takes them for granted. But Hugo had never ceased to
marvel at the age he lived in – it had too much of the
flavour of a turning point – forwards or backwards, whichever, it had to be recognised and respected. And, above all,
understood.

It wasn't until he arrived at the high wire fence that he
remembered there were two entrances. He plumped for the
first and turned left. At the gate, he was, to his mild
surprise, expected.

'Dr Brill,' said the guard, with a respectful nod. 'Please
park across there, sir.'

Hugo parked to the left of a wide turning area, and as he
got out of his car he saw a pleasant-looking, grey-haired
man approaching him from another car parked across the
way.

'Dr Brill, this is a great pleasure,' he said.

'Indeed it is,' said Hugo.

'My name is Barnes.' He turned to indicate the security lodge. 'Well, let's get you checked in, and we'll be on our way.'

Inside the small brick building, a very different guard greeted him, a steely smile letting Hugo know that Dr Brill or no Dr Brill, he ought really to frisk him for a Luger. He was asked to sign a security chit and keep it on him, whilst the guard pinned a small badge marked 'Visitor' on his lapel. Now for the fingerprints, thought Hugo, but Barnes rescued him and took him outside into the sunshine.

'We'll go in your car,' he said. 'I'll show you the way.'

It was difficult, driving and looking, wanting to ask questions about everything, not wanting to appear too inquisitive. They were passing the two huge buildings topped by the lighthouses, even more impressive at close quarters.

'What are those?' asked Hugo.

'Oh, that is the very first Windscale plant, built between '48 and '50 for atomic weapon research.'

'Weapon research?' murmured Hugo. 'Is it still in operation?'

'No, used for offices now.' Barnes looked at him. 'I had the great pleasure of meeting your wife, Dr Brill.'

'Ah,' said Hugo.

'On many occasions.' Barnes laughed. 'Doesn't pull her punches. She went over the plant with a fine-tooth comb. I can't wait to see what she's written about us.'

'Was she here yesterday, Mr Barnes?'

'No. Turn left here, and straight on.'

They were passing the huge silver sphere.

'What is that incredible thing?' said Hugo, craning to look.

'AGR – Advanced Gas-Cooled Reactor. No, Dr Brill,

she was here the day before yesterday, and seemed to have all she wanted. I gather she's gone back to London and you've missed each other.'

News travels fast, thought Hugo.

'Just follow the road round, Dr Brill.'

They crossed the railway line, passing between tanks and buildings of all shapes and sizes, but Hugo barely noticed. He was trying to find the words that would lead him to Jenny.

'Did she actually say she was going to London, Mr Barnes?'

'No. No, she just said "Mr Barnes, I think I've got it," and she left.'

'She said that to you the day before yesterday but she was still at the hotel yesterday morning because she called me.' Hugo shook his head. 'She didn't say where she was going?'

'No. Ah, left turn here.' They were travelling alongside what seemed to be a canal. 'This is the River Calder, its course has been straightened where it passes through the works. Now, right turn over the bridge.'

Ahead loomed two of the massive cooling towers, rising above them like mountain peaks as they drove around and came to the front of a long central building.

'This is Calder Hall, Dr Brill. The administration block. You can park across the way, just there.'

As they walked back across the road, a small man in a white coat came out to meet them.

'McLaren, this is Dr Brill. I'll leave him with you. Enjoy your tour, sir.'

Barnes disappeared into the building and McLaren shook hands.

'Good morning, Dr Brill, you've chosen a nice day.'

It was a glorious day, the sun bright and warm, picking out the shining metal segments that thrust out in spirals

52

and right-angles from the bizarre structures, topped with pairs of skinny black plant stacks, to their left.

'This is the Calder Works, the world's first industrial nuclear power station, opened in October, 1956. These are the two turbine halls, each fed by two Magnox gas-cooled reactors, and there are two cooling towers at each end.'

'Ah,' said Hugo. 'The odd-shaped buildings are the reactors – and there are four at work.'

'Yes, sir. We produce 180 megawatts of electricity. When one is being serviced, the others keep the turbines in operation.'

They walked in silence for a minute or two, and Hugo saw some herring gulls, screaming and fighting over scraps of food. They reminded him of his apprehensions last night when he drove around the compound. But whatever was in the fish they ate, they seemed to be thriving well enough. No destruction of wild life here, then, and that after twenty-two years of operation. It was all so different by day. All so clean and clinical, no filthy coal-yards and gasworks, no grime and dust polluting the Cumberland air, as it did in the coal-mining areas north of Whitehaven. He found himself respectful, admiring.

'It's all very clean,' he said, 'apart from the smoke in these monsters.'

'Steam, sir, steam,' said McLaren smiling, 'condensing back into water.'

Of course! The sinister plumes – the ominous tapestries of doom weaving across the sky – even these were no more than spouts of innocent steam. He should have known that! Nothing here for Jenny to snap up and use in evidence against! McLaren indicated that they turn left towards one of the Magnox buildings.

'I don't know how much you know about these things, Dr Brill, but I'll keep it as simple as possible.'

Good, thought Hugo, peripheral knowledge is a snare.

53

I do know roughly how they work, but why tell you what I know; I want to find out what you know. I shall confine myself to a few incredibly intelligent questions.

'What are these?' said Hugo, composing his first gem, pointing to the ramshackle structures on each corner of the building.

'Heat exchangers.' McLaren pointed upwards. 'The reactor core goes right up through the centre of the building. The energy released by fission is mostly in the form of heat, about 400 degrees Centigrade. A coolant of carbon dioxide gas passes through the core and transfers the heat through those heat exchangers to produce steam. This is fed to the turbines to generate electricity.'

'Carbon dioxide coolant, hence "Gas Cooled",' said Hugo, excelling himself. 'The fast breeder coolant is *liquid* sodium, so it's not *gas* cooled.'

'Exactly,' said McLaren, giving Hugo an 'A' and an old-fashioned look.

They went into the building and McLaren pressed the button on a large services lift with folding doors. They arrived at the top and went through into a huge room, taking up the full extent of the building and entirely deserted. He led Hugo across to the centre of the floor, and stood beside him on an enormous grill with seven sides, studded with great nuts, like a jumbo-sized Solitaire. He smiled.

'You are now, Dr Brill, standing exactly on top of the nuclear reactor.'

Hugo looked at him and smiled back, unable to see the joke. He was standing on top – *on top* – of the nuclear reactor. Was it happening now, he thought, this instant? The insidious attack upon his cellular structure, the slow, silent, unspeakable death by ionising radiation? Thus, he thought, feels the jungle savage, helpless before the Witch Doctor's curse. Herewith walks the green recruit, pulling the pin from his first hand grenade. I have to face the fact, he told himself, that this is something I have never experienced before in my whole life and I want to get the hell off it as soon as possible!

Red notices, informing interested parties that radiation was below the Maximum Permissible Dose of 5 rem per year, did little to reassure him; after all, the MPD was for those occupationally exposed to radiation and the Dose Limit for the public was one tenth, 500 millirem, another good reason, felt Hugo, as a member of the public, not to linger. Yet he found himself listening with excessive politeness as McLaren told him that the nuclear core was, in fact, shielded with steel-lined concrete, many feet thick, to protect operators and the public from neutrons and gamma radiation; that beneath the grill was a lattice of vertical channels made of graphite, which moderated the speed of the travelling neutrons so they could hit the niggardly supply of uranium-235 isotopes and produce fission; that through this same grill were lowered the control rods of steel, containing boron which absorbed neutrons and slowed down the reaction to keep it at a critical level. McLaren lingered, oh, how McLaren lingered on every detail of these fascinating little facts, and Hugo was yearning to tell him that he had read about them already in the glorious immunity of his study and could they please move on. More to come. McLaren explained how the mobile, remote-controlled superstructures on tracks were used to raise the spent fuel and charge the core with new fuel in the form of rods encased in a magnesium alloy called Magnox.

'Ah, Magnox!' Hugo cleared his throat noisily. 'Hence, Magnox gas-cooled reactors.'

'Exactly,' said McLaren. He paused a moment, thinking what he had missed, then, oh blessed relief, he was leading Hugo through another door and out of the Witch's Crucible into an antichamber where hand monitors and showers were installed to protect the personnel. 'Only necessary when engaged on maintenance or decontamination work,' said McLaren, and was off before Hugo had time to say 'What about us?'

They were out on the landing, descending the stairs to the next level. The room below was sinister in a different way, a long, thin antichamber, curving in an arc around the central core, that omnipotent, omnipresent reactor on the other side of the wall. This time, he wasn't on top of it, he was at the side of it. Maybe the radiation went sideways? The room was filled with cabinets, monitors and more pipes, the triple fail-safe mechanisms that kept the whole thing from doing something very nasty to the west coast of Cumberland. And, again, not a soul in sight.

On the next flight of stairs, Hugo dared to ask where all the personnel were working.

'The whole unit is operated by five men,' said McLaren.

'Only five nuclear physicists to run all this?'

'Not nuclear physicists, Dr Brill. Just ordinary workmen, trained to operate and service the instruments. Now here we come to the central control room, the master computer that does all the work.'

A solitary man was sitting silent at a console, watching a wall covered with dials and monitors and flashing lights, knobs and switches and plugs and fuses, one solitary man in charge of the computer in charge of the core wherein was burning the fire of Prometheus. Is this what Jenny meant when she said 'I've got it', thought Hugo, because I think I've got more than I want of it! What happens if he faints or has a seizure? His fears were calmed when another man came in with a small box. Well, at least someone was around, some of the time, watching the man who was watching the wall.

After two or three years of Hugo's life, they were outside

on the path once more, back in the blazing sunshine. He began to think straight again. He had imagined a spacious, bustling control room, filled with boffins and atomic scientists, nuclear physicists and back-room boys. Not the whole thing run by five semi-skilled technicians, trained to check the nuts and bolts! Dad's Army holding back the Wehrmacht!

They followed the fat pipes carrying steam from the heat exchangers into the Turbine Hall. Here, Hugo was treated to Chaplin's *Modern Times* in glorious Technicolour, mammoth turbines painted in primary colours, prodigal splashes of red or blue or yellow, spotless floors, gleaming, polished brass, all admirably ship-shape and obviously run, Hugo guessed, by a horde of ex-Navy charladies. They passed along a high cat-walk, through a door, down some stairs, into the administration hall, out on to the sunny front porch, and were back where they had started.

That was it! That was all! Calder Hall! A miracle, operated by computers, nursed by five technicians. Incredibly dangerous? Insane? Or magnificently simple? And safe?

'Mr McLaren,' he said, making up his mind, 'thank you. I think that the critics of nuclear power should come here and see it for themselves. I think they might shut up and cheer!'

'Well, they have given us a bit of stick, lately,' said McLaren, looking quite relieved, 'but I'm proud of it.'

'Of course,' said Hugo, and felt a twinge. He was being disloyal to Jenny. But he could not discount the miraculous ease, the economy and the cleanliness of the nuclear station; he could see no way that she could discredit the entire nuclear power programme at this level.

The question of environmental pollution and irradiation was another issue. The Parker Report had spelled it out – there was no secret here, in fact it had all been notoriously publicised – permanent waste storage was the major stumbling block in the nuclear bid to become the power-house of the future. First, the spent fuel rods, highly radioactive, were stored to cool in ponds, then barely stripped in time before the Magnox cladding corroded – next, the valuable uranium, plutonium and sundry fission products were stored for re-use. But what then to do with the lethal residue? Highly active liquid waste, stored in tanks, which might nurse a propensity to crack. Low active liquid waste discharged into the Irish Sea, and let the fish work it out for themselves. Low active gas waste sent sky-wards, via the plant stacks, and ending up in somebody's milk. Low active solid waste buried in trenches at Drigg, and God help the dog that thinks he's found a bone. And of course, medium active solid waste stored in metal cannisters for burial at sea; the cannisters corrode, release the lethal contents, and bingo! Monster crabs and giant shrimps join the hordes of gargantuan ants marching through the pages of science fiction. Truly, a nightmare of uneasy possibilities, far too many fussy, infuriating ways to bury the indes-tructible poison. But all these dangers under increasing surveillance, monitored, open to criticism. And none of them, in any way, to be assessed on a layman's tour of one or two brief visits, without instruments, meters or expert knowledge.

And yet, the day before yesterday, Jenny had said to Barnes 'I think I've got it.' Yesterday, she had called Hugo up in a state of obvious excitement, to say the story was more than she'd hoped. And yesterday, she had gone missing! Why?

Chapter Six

Barnes appeared again. Hugo shook hands with McLaren and thanked him. Barnes took him back to his car.

'I'll see you round to the main gate, Dr Brill. What did you think of it?'

'Incredible. Quite incredible.' As Hugo pulled out on to the perimeter road leading back down to the gate, he saw another car come up close behind, felt a moment of unease, wondered why he was being followed, then realised it was Barnes's chauffeur.

'Mr Barnes, did you conduct my wife around Calder Hall?'

'Yes, Dr Brill.'

'Did she make any comment, ask to see anything else?'

'Yes, indeed she did!' Barnes laughed. 'She wanted to see everything. Normally we limit our tours to Calder Hall, because we haven't the staff to spare.' No, thought Hugo, they're all too busy watching each other. 'But occasionally we can manage it in additional visits. Your wife was here four times.'

'What else did she see?'

'Ah. She saw the Advanced Gas-Cooled Reactor, very similar in principle but with higher temperatures than the Magnox; it turns out thirty-three megawatts but it is interesting mainly because it was the first AGR prototype to be built – that was in '62. Five more have been under construction for ten years –' He frowned and shook his head. 'But this is still the only AGR to have gone critical.'

'Nothing else?'

'Yes.' He paused and looked at Hugo for a moment. 'She wanted to see the old Windscale plant.'

They turned a corner, and there it was coming up on their left, the two towering buildings, the giant chimneys rising up like lighthouses, the highest structures on the whole site.

'Why would she be interested in a block of offices, Mr Barnes?'

'I have no idea whatsoever, Dr Brill. Pull up here, please.

Hugo parked near the security lodge and tried to recall something he had read in the Parker Report under the heading, 'Public Hostility'. Of course! One of these original Windscale reactors had been destroyed by fire in 1957! And Justice Parker had gone to great lengths to discredit a documentary film that was admitted to be a mock-up of the Windscale fire with clips drawn from other sources. Why a mock-up, mused Hugo, were there no genuine newsreel clips?

'Mr Barnes?' Hugo found himself reasoning in Jenny's place. 'Was she interested in the fire here in 1957?'

Barnes looked at him again for a moment, smiled and nodded.

'Yes, she did ask about that.'

He opened the car door and Hugo got out, too, still pressing.

'And she would have wanted to know why the·e were

60

no visible signs of damage, why the buildings had been converted to offices, and, indeed, why the whole place had not been demolished and redeveloped in the last twenty-one years.' Barnes shut the door and looked at his watch. 'Well, Mr Barnes?'

'Uneconomic, sir. The available funds were used on the development of Calder Hall, barely opened when the fire occurred.' He went on quickly. 'You have the uncanny habit of asking the same questions as your wife, Dr Brill. Are you sure you haven't discussed it with her in the last few days?'

'No, Mr Barnes. I haven't seen her since she came up here two weeks ago, and I have no idea where she is now.'

'Really?' Barnes seemed hardly convinced. 'Well, I can understand your concern, Dr Brill. But she's probably gone back to London. She had all she wanted from us and left.'

'But what did she want? Did she look over the old plant?'

'Some of it.'

'Can I see it too, Mr Barnes?'

Just for a moment, Hugo caught the same look, in Barnes's eyes, that he had seen in the eyes of the hotel receptionist, looking away as if to check with somebody in authority. Then the same smile, a brief look at his watch, and Barnes nodded.

'A quick tour, Dr Brill; I have a lunch appointment at twelve o'clock.'

They walked rapidly towards the nearer of the two buildings and Hugo saw that they were H-shaped, about one hundred yards apart and separated by a long administration block, set back in line with the plant stacks. Each building was about three hundred feet in length, two hundred deep.

'What was actually inside here, Mr Barnes?'

'The first Windscale reactors, Piles 1 and 2. They opened

in 1952 to produce fissile plutonium for nuclear weapons. After the '57 fire, the function of Piles 1 and 2 was transferred to the Calder Hall reactors.'

'I see. These reactors, or Piles, were built between 1948 and 1950 and started up in 1952. Calder Hall started up in 1956 and Piles 1 and 2 closed down in 1957. Twenty-one years ago!'

Barnes laughed as he motioned Hugo through the large doors into a surprisingly small entrance hall; in one corner a desk faced them, behind it a uniformed man nodded to Barnes. A large notice-board on the wall to his left was chequered with office memos and posters.

'Well put, Dr Brill, you have it, dates and all.'

Dates and all! Yes, the dates intrigued Hugo and he knew they would have intrigued Jenny. But why? No matter, he had them in his head and they would bounce themselves around the antechambers until the cerebral computer was ready to deliver them up, all sorted out into significant relationships. In all his research projects, Hugo had never once doubted this would happen. He just fed in the facts and waited.

Barnes led him through a door to the right of the reception hall and they walked along the outer corridor, passing office doors on their left at brief and regular intervals.

'All quite ordinary, I'm afraid,' said Barnes, 'accounts, wages, personnel, typing pools and, inevitably, tea-makers.'

'Five to run a reactor and fifty to keep them there?'

Barnes laughed again and seemed to relax for the first time.

'Parkinson's Law, Dr Brill.'

'Well put, Mr Barnes.'

They turned right, then left, following the leg of the 'H'. One of the doors opened as they passed and a girl came out, carrying a sheaf of papers. Hugo smiled at her and looked past her into the office. It was rather like looking into a single room without bath at a five-star hotel. Sumptuous entrance halls, priceless chandeliers, flower shops, gourmet restaurants, carpeted stairways, astronomical charges – you open your door, and barely room to swing a poodle! But the veteran traveller keeps his cell in the Grand Hotel and walks around as if he owns a suite. How many veteran travellers here? thought Hugo.

He checked other doors that were open, kept checking as they turned left into another corridor that ran two hundred feet to the back of the immense block. How odd! The offices were all stuck on the outside of the building like the pieces of a mosaic, just as the control rooms at Calder Hall had been imprisoned in that semi-circle around the reactor. He couldn't resist the next question.

'What's inside now, Mr Barnes?'

But Barnes kept walking, reached halfway and paused at an opening that turned right into a glass-panelled corridor, leading away from the 'H' block towards the long building in the centre of the complex.

'I'll just take you into the old admin. and research section then I'm afraid I shall have to leave you.' He made to walk on and Hugo stopped him.

'Mr Barnes! What's inside all this now? The offices barely take up more than a narrow slice on the outside of this immense building. Like inhabiting the shell of an egg.'

Barnes turned and looked at him, looked at his watch, and this time he was clearly thinking very hard. He spoke at last.

'Why, Dr Brill, there is nothing inside. The shell is empty.'

Hugo screwed up his eyes and looked back along the corridor, speaking slowly.

'You mean that the reactor and the plant – everything inside there – was destroyed . . . and then left? Just left, for twenty-one years?'

'Both reactors were filled in with concrete. The rest of the plant was sealed off after the fire in case of contamination, checked and cleared and declared safe but obsolescent. The outer corridor was converted into offices on each level, and, as I did say before, until the Ministry provides the cash to rationalise the use of the space, we make the best of what we have. This way, please.'

Hugo followed him in silence, looking back through the panelled glass windows at the huge block behind them, his eyes climbing the walls of the ghost plant that reached up far above, following the dead chimney that soared even higher to the tombstone structure at the top. He was suddenly aware that he was experiencing a kind of fear, something akin to the dread he had felt when he was actually on top of the Calder Hall reactor, perhaps the way a diver feels when he circuits the wreck of a sunken galleon. And he hadn't the faintest idea why!

They were coming into the central administration block, bustling and busy and spacious and normal. Now he began to feel like an absolute idiot. It was all getting out of hand, ordinary things were taking on sinister overtones, he really must apologise to poor old Barnes. Fancy, Dr Brill, acting like a bloody crank, you ought to know better!

But Barnes was consulting his watch with more than a hint of impatience.

'It's after twelve, Dr Brill, and I always insist on punctuality. Will you excuse me while I make my apologies, a quick 'phone call then I'll see you to your car.' He indicated a door marked 'Waiting Room'.

'I really am terribly sorry, Mr Barnes, I had no idea,' said Hugo, and went inside.

The room was pleasantly furnished, some plastic armchairs, a coffee-table with the mandatory magazine supplements from the *Observer* and the *Sunday Times*, framed prints of Cumberland scenes on the plain white walls. Hugo dropped into one of the chairs and lit a cigarette. He puffed on it a couple of times, then, still preoccupied, stubbed it out in a sand-tray beside his chair.

'Oh, blast, I've done that bloody thing again!' he growled, and shoved the ugly, bent cigarette deep into the sand to hide it from sight. As he did so, he stirred up the end of another cigarette that had been covered over. He stroked the sand away and jiggled the other stub to the surface. It was barely smoked, bent in the middle.

And it was Benson and Hedges, tipped.

Jenny's brand.

Chapter Seven

When Barnes came back, he found Hugo crouched forward in his chair, hands covering his eyes. Hugo followed him to the security lodge, handed back his visitor's badge and pass, shook hands, thanked him profusely, apologised for delaying his lunch, and drove off. When he had turned right, away from the wire fence, and traversed the apologetic little dual carriageway that went each side of a clump of bushes and between a cluster of small houses, Hugo pulled up at the first available lay-by.

He sat a moment, then took his handkerchief from his breast pocket and unwrapped it very slowly, like a man in a trance. The two rumpled fag-ends were lying side by side. One was his. And the other was Jenny's. It had to be. Who else at Windscale had such ugly habits? Who else puffed Benson and Hedges tipped, twice, and stubbed them out? Wait! It was in the visitors' room. Who else, *visiting* Windscale, puffed Benson and Hedges tipped, twice, and stubbed them out? He wrapped them carefully again and put them away. It was Jenny's cigarette.

In itself, it meant nothing. The day before yesterday, let's get the days right, that was Tuesday, she had waited in that room. What of it? Just another of the niggling little minutiae that were popping up all over the place, everywhere Jenny had been. Popping up, because the trail was still hot, because he had decided on impulse to drive up to Cumberland on Wednesday, the very day she disappeared. Popping up, because nobody had bothered to clear away the used soap at the Cold Pike Hotel, empty the sand-tray in the Windscale Visitors' Room. Popping up, because people still remembered exactly what Jenny did and what she said. A week later, it would all have been covered up – and he would have had nothing in his mind but the distrust and jealousy and pain that had driven him after her all the way to Cumberland. Well, now he was free of such doubts. But what was in their place? Where, damn it, was it all leading him?

... *brrr – ting – Operation Cerebral Computer – brrr – the receptionist had hesitated – brrr – Jenny hadn't taken the soap brrr – his briefcase had, repeat,* had *been moved – brrr – the restaurant manager hadn't seen her suitcase – brrr – the Swede hadn't seen the suitcase – brrr – Check Suit had seen the suitcase-brrr-brrr-brrr – Jenny interested in the block of offices – brrr-ting – Jenny interested in the Windscale Fire – brrr-ting – Barnes ... Barnes ... Barnes, something elusive in his manner – brrr – the offices pinned to the wall like a mosaic, what's inside now, Mr Barnes? – brrr-brrr – Jenny's cigarette in the tray – brrr-brrr – Jenny disappeared! – ting-buzz-brrrrrrr – here it comes – read it out, Hugo ...*

'My God!' He gripped the steering wheel and looked up at the sky, shaking his head, 'It can't be a bloody conspiracy!' He started the engine. 'You are definitely cracking up, old boy! Illuminatus rules the world? Oh dear, oh dear! Things can happen for very ordinary reasons, you know that, Brill?

'Yes, but –'

'Start driving and think straight! You are definitely getting paranoid.'

He began driving back to the hotel, thinking about his next move. If he had packed his bag he could have gone straight for the M6 and been back in London by evening. Sweet, lovely London. Innocent, normal London, where Jenny was probably sprawled out in the study at home, feet up, writing up the Windscale Fire of 1957 in lurid colours.

'TRAGEDY IN OLD WINDSCALE, WHAT GREATER TRAGEDY LIES AHEAD IN NEW GEHENNA!'

'WHAT NEXT IN NUCLEAR GAME OF FISSION ROULETTE? READ "ATOMS" FOR "BULLETS", WHOSE FINGER ON THE TRIGGER?'

'That bloody cigarette!' He shouted it out loud. 'It doesn't mean a damned thing! She buried it in the ashtray on Tuesday, she called me at eleven-thirty on Wednesday, left at twelve, went where? Not back to Windscale –'

Hugo braked sharply. He was driving too fast, not even looking back at the plumes of steam behind him.

'Why not back to Windscale?'

'What was that?'

'Lateral thinking, Hugo, let us take her back to Windscale.'

'But that means –"

'Right! She went back to Windscale yesterday, left the cigarette in the waiting-room yesterday.'

'That's Wednesday.'

'Correct! She saw Barnes yesterday as well as the day before, when he said he last saw her.'

'Which was Tuesday.'

'Therefore, Barnes is lying today!'

'Thursday.'

'Brilliant! It's a pleasure to talk to you, Hugo.'

'For God's sake, Brill –'

'Now! We have two possible liars, Barnes and Check Suit, who said she *took* her suitcase – brrr-brrr-bingo! Two possible liars make a possible conspiracy.'

Hugo switched on the car radio. He wished Dr Brill, Ph.D., had stayed behind in London. The prepared mind can be a very persistent beast. Somebody was talking about trade unions without affection. He half listened. At least it took his mind off the obsessive track that was stifling his common sense in an airless universe of dead reactors and missing wives. Not an ounce of proof, just a series of small incidents running round and round in his mind.

It was one o'clock as he approached the Cold Pike Hotel, under the railway arch, up the incline.

'This is the one o'clock news. After an all-night search, helped by three hundred neighbours, the body of three-year-old Janet Lane was found in a school playground, half a mile from her home. She had been the victim of a frenzied knife attack. Police have –'

Hugo switched off with a groan of horror and disbelief.

'Jesus! What a bloody world! Three years old!' He drove into the forecourt of the hotel, stopped the car and sat for a moment, looking at nothing. 'Oh, God, where are you, Jenny?' A deep sadness was in him. But at least he knew now what he had to do. With a sudden effort of will, he braced himself and went into the hotel. The phone booth was empty. He called home collect, closed his eyes for sixteen timeless burrs, and lowered the receiver. He took a deep breath, held it a moment, exhaled fast and called the offices of *Change!*, collect, person to person, Jeremy Wright, editor. It was accepted.

'Jeremy, a thousand apologies, deduct the call from Jenny's salary, but it's urgent. Two things! Has she contacted you in the last couple of days?'

'Why yes, Hugo love, she called me yesterday morning.'

69

'She did? What time?'

'Ah! Um – about – eleven o'clock – eleven-fifteen! Sounded very excited, which is not unusual for your dear wife, and wanted impossible, instant information by this morning.'

'But she didn't call back this morning?'

'No.'

'Did she say what she was up to? Where she was going?'

'No, old lad, she likes to surprise me.'

'Yes, well, I'm up here in Cumberland, I came up here yesterday to surprise *her* and she isn't here. Booked out of the hotel at midday.'

'Well, no panic, Hugo, she's obviously on the scent of some mind-boggling revelation that will transmogrify the cosmos; isn't she always?'

'I hope to God you're right, Jeremy.' Jeremy Wright, the eternal undergraduate, always so darned flippant, but he was making Hugo feel better by the minute. 'Listen! I won't keep you much longer, don't sweat. Can you find out something for me? I want the details, news clippings, newsreel coverage, anything, on the big fire at the first Windscale plant in 1957. It broke out in one of the original reactors. I want to find out all there is – and oh, yes, how much it was played down in the national press – 1957!'

There was silence on the other end. Hugo had a sudden fear he had been cut off, spoke again quickly.

'Hello! Hello! Jeremy! I hope they haven't cut you off the damned line!'

'Well ... that is ... bloody incredible.' Jeremy was speaking again slowly, seemed to be amused. 'Incredible. You say you haven't seen Jenny?' He began to laugh. 'But that is exactly what she asked me to find out for her yesterday morning!'

70

Hugo had read her mind! He had divined the only way she could discredit the new plant, linking it with the breakdown of the old plant in 1957!

'Jeremy, this is not funny, it's vital! It proves I was on the right track. I think there was a disaster in 1957, something so big that the Government had to cover it up. I think there was a conspiracy at a high level and Jenny is on to it. It could explain an awful lot. Did you find out anything?'

'Oh yes, indeed I did!' The bloody fool still sounded amused. 'I have some truly earth-shattering results which will set you right back on your clever old academic ear. I sent Paul to Colindale to check the Cumbrian and national press.'

'Well tell me, for God's sake, was it a big disaster?'

'Horrendous, old lad, in its sublunary significance! They poured two million litres of milk into the sea!'

The line went dead at both ends for a giant five seconds.

'They – did – *what*?' Hugo was undone. Jeremy was ecstatic.

'They poured all the bloody milk for miles around into the rivers and the sea, old lad. The media had a week of Schadenfreude. You see, the fire released a vast cloud of radio-isotopes via the plant stacks, but, thanks to the filters installed on top, the boffins said that only one of them, iodine-131, was any kind of hazard to human health. It fell all over the fells for miles around and cattle grazing in the fields produced milk-shakes with radio-iodine flavour of the month. So they poured it all away! The Great Yoghurt Disaster of 1957!'

'That's – all?'

'Well, there was a witty little couplet:

> "*The rivers and creeks*
> *Stank of sour milk for weeks*"

71

and a cartoon of a local fish being caught, already served up with hollandaise sauce. I'm afraid your conspiracy at a high level was just one big national joke, old boy.'

'That's all there was? No other radio-isotopes released, no other effects on the local population?'

'A lot of farmers got rich. From the compensation paid out, the local cows must have produced more milk in a month than United Dairies sold in a year. But cheer up, old lad, Paul is checking Hansard for contemporary questions in Parliament, and I'll have something on news-reel coverage by tomorrow.'

'Yes.' Hugo had lost heart, wondered how Jenny would take it. 'I'll be back home today, and come in to see you in the morning. And conspiracy or no conspiracy, if Jenny isn't home by then, I'm going to start things moving. Peter Marion's at the Environment, I'll get him on to it.'

'Won't be necessary, Hugo, she's somewhere doing something splendid. See you tomorrow! Cheers!'

'Cheers.'

Hugo put the 'phone down. It was time to go home. He could alert the local police, no harm in that, she might have had a very ordinary accident. But first he must pack and book out – probably have to pay for another day, it was one-fifteen. As he moved towards the stairs, he glanced through the door leading to the bar.

Check Suit was sitting there with another man. He saw Hugo, leapt to his feet, beaming, and waved him to come through. 'What the hell,' muttered Hugo to himself, but he went.

'My dear Dr Brill, what a pleasant surprise, I thought you'd gone. Er – my partner, Ernest Rogers – and do you know I don't think I actually introduced myself last night. My name is Fallon. George Fallon.'

Hugo shook hands with him, then with his partner, a tall, heavily-built man with a smile that didn't reach his eyes, and a grip that brought tears to Hugo's. What is this? thought Hugo, he looks like Jack Pallance; Fallon looks like David Niven. Some estate agency – Niven charms the clients, Pallance beats 'em up! Who am I playing, Paul Henreid? When does Peter Lorre come in?

'Sit down,' said Fallon, 'What will you have?'

Hugo, about to excuse himself, glanced down, noticed they were having a light lunch of crusty bread, cheese, pickled onions and beer, and felt peckish. He had a journey ahead of him. Fallon didn't miss a trick.

'Johnny!' he called to the barman. The Swede wasn't on this shift. 'Same again! Bread, cheese, beer – and a pickle, eh?' His eyes crinkled with mirth, then were suddenly serious. 'Your wife, Dr Brill. Any news?'

'I'm afraid not, Mr Fallon.' Hugo's heart was not in it. 'No news at all.'

'Oh, I am sorry. But I'm sure she's quite safe. I hear you went to Calder Hall this morning. Impressive, isn't it?'

'It is indeed. Incredibly clean. I think that impressed me most.'

'The thing of the future, don't doubt it – keep your North Sea Oil and Scottish Independence – the almighty atom has all the energy we'll ever need.'

'So long as it's safely under control.'

'Well, we're still here, eh, Ernie?' Fallon roared and Ernie almost smiled again.

The food and beer were brought and Fallon paid, waving Hugo to silence. Hugo was hungry. He buttered the bread, laid on a hunk of cheese and crunched into it. The others chomped away, ravenous, sharing the noise, feeding time at the Zoo.

'Well, Dr Brill,' said Fallon, biting into a pickled onion, 'what are your plans now?'

Hugo took a huge swig at his beer and looked at the wall clock. It was one-thirty already. 'I'm going back to

London this afternoon. If I leave by two I could be home by eight o'clock.'

'More likely nine o'clock,' beamed Fallon.

Hugo nodded, then remembered. First he had to sort out the County police. 'Do you know,' he buttered some more bread, 'where I can find the local police station?'

His eyes came up to Fallon in the split second that Fallon's eyes moved to his – and the look that Fallon had exchanged with Rogers was still in them – a look of surprising intelligence – and concern.

'Ye – es.' His eyes crinkled back into vacuous humour. 'Follow the high street, bearing left from the hotel.' He had finished eating. 'You are still worried about your wife?'

'I called home a few minutes ago and there was no answer. I called her office and she was supposed to call them this morning and didn't. I think I should at least alert the police this end before I leave.'

'Of course, of course.' He looked at Ernie. 'No harm at all. Except the County police will only scout around up here, and she may be back in London, anywhere, by now.'

'Yes.' Ernie suddenly spoke up with an incongruously well-modulated voice, the inflections of a sergeant-major taking tea at the Ritz. 'But I can tell you what they'll say as of now, sir. They will inform you that if there is no suspicion of danger, if it may be assumed that she has left normally, even run away, for her own purposes, it is her business and the police are not bound to investigate.'

'How do we know there is no suspicion of danger?'

'We don't, sir. But if she did not leave her luggage behind at the hotel – and I gather she took her suitcase – and, er, is over seventeen, then the local police will tell you precisely that.'

'He should know,' Fallon nodded with a grimace of respect, 'he used to be one of them.'

I'll bet he did, thought Hugo, and I don't see him selling

houses. The spark of suspicion was rekindling within him, overcoming his despair at Jeremy's news. Ernie knows about the suitcase, so Fallon has been talking – the two of them happen to be here when I come back – Barnes made a 'phone call before I left. Heaven help me, I may very well be cracking up under the strain. I may need to drive away on the open road and let the stench of sour milk waft away in the slipstream. I may then realise that I have been grossly over-reacting, but, oh dear me, Hugo, it could be a conspiracy. It *could* be!

'Well,' said Hugo, standing up and looking carefully at the two men. 'Scotland Yard have a National Register of Missing Persons. And if my wife isn't home by tomorrow, or very soon after, I have a few well-muscled contacts at a higher level, and that, thank God, is one of the rare benefits of being a university don!'

There, thought Hugo, take a nice, crunchy bite out of that with your pickled onions. If you are both what you say, you'll think I am merely over-anxious and a little pompous. But if you are checking me out for your own bloody purposes, then that will leave you with a couple of straight lefts to the beer belly.

He shook hands with them and thanked Fallon for the meal.

'Not at all, Dr Brill.' David Niven was back. 'And good luck.'

Jack Pallance crushed his hand once more, and nodded.

Paul Henreid smiled and walked from the bar. He had struck a blow for the freedom fighters, and à bas les aristos!

Upstairs, Clark Kent packed with super speed, left the room with a long sigh of relief, paid his bill with a flicker of satisfaction when he wasn't charged for an extra day, and realised that he was actually feeling quite pleased with himself. One way or another, he was having an effect on this inscrutable environment. He was sure that Jenny was not up here exploring her navel with a new-found guru. And now he had this feeling that he had involved himself with whatever danger she might be in. Danger! An ugly word. Please God, it was all a dream.

As he passed the bar, he saw that Fallon and Rogers had left. He saw that their beer glasses were half-full and wasn't at all surprised.

It was still a nice day outside. He went to the car and put his suitcase in the tailgate. He walked round to the driver's door and noticed that a black Cortina was parked a few yards away. There were two men inside. As he opened his door, one of the men climbed out and walked across to him.

'Dr Brill?'

Hugo's heart was thumping. He found himself looking round, saw there was nobody else in sight, wondered if a quick dash back into the hotel might not be the wisest course. But, like the man sitting in the barber's chair, watching someone take his coat through the mirror, he did nothing.

'Yes,' he said.

'I have a message from Mr Barnes at Windscale. He would like to see you. He may have news of your wife.'

'Oh! Oh, that's wonderful,' said Hugo. 'Where is she? Is she safe?'

'Mr Barnes will tell you personally. It will be much simpler if you will accompany me, I can take you straight to him, we have clearance at the gate, then I can bring you back.'

'Yes, well – er – alright,' said Hugo, and walked round the Cortina. The other man got out; Hugo climbed in next to the man with clearance at the gate, the other man closed the car door, and walked into the hotel.

'Isn't he coming too?' asked Hugo ineptly.

'I just dropped him off, he has business in town.'

They were pulling away from the hotel, and Hugo wondered if Jenny had been picked up the same way. So simple, so reasonable, one doesn't even ask for identification. One to drive her off, one to go back and pack her bag, clean up all trace, not notice the sliver of soap, square things with the receptionist, the manager, the car hire company. Whatever doubts he had before, the conspiracy hypothesis was taking precedence over alternatives. But Hugo also knew that he was going, without protest, for another reason.

This quasi-abduction was something new, something dramatically out of the ordinary, a qualitative step beyond the matter of fact minutiae that had obsessed him until now. Now he was in James Bond country, picked up by a man in a black Cortina, wondering how effective his refusal might have been. Would they have used force?

He let his hand rest lightly on the door trim, close to the handle. At the first sign of a detour away from the route to Windscale, he would leap out and cry for help – if there was anyone about – if the car wasn't going too fast!

But the journey was uneventful. The plumes of innocent steam soon appeared and beckoned them back to the plant, welcomed them, turning left at the high wire fence, and ushered them through the main gate. No pause here, the security man nodded, and Hugo relaxed. It was all genuine, all normal, all safe.

They drove to the front of the admin. block and parked.

'This way, sir,' said the man with clearance, and led Hugo into the entrance hall, past the door marked 'Waiting Room' to a lift entrance that he hadn't noticed on his first visit. The man put a key into a small lock and the lift doors opened. Aha, thought Hugo, a private lift! The man closed the door, pressed a button, and to Hugo's astonishment the lift went down! Down? Where, dear Lord, is down? The doors opened again and they were facing a dimly-lit, cement-lined corridor that led off somewhere into the distance. The man indicated that they go straight ahead, and Hugo judged that they were actually walking parallel to the old Windscale plant, skirting the old reactor building. Did Jenny come this way? Is this what had happened to the poor kid?

The man stopped at a door and pushed a bell.

'Come in!' called a familiar voice.

The man stepped aside and ushered Hugo in alone. It was another small room – they really conserved space in this obsolescent lighthouse. There was a desk in the centre, an empty chair in front of it. And three men.

Jack Pallance was leaning against the far wall, his arms folded. Mr Barnes was sitting at the desk, nodding a solemn welcome. And beside him was the other man – the man in the check suit with the David Niven moustache.

'Sit down, Dr Brill,' said Fallon.

Chapter Eight

'Now, Dr Brill,' said Fallon, 'I need hardly say we are not estate agents. I suspect you were on to us over the cheese and pickles. So let's start all over again. I am Major Fallon, and I am responsible for all security measures and surveillance at Calder Hall and Windscale. My good friend, Commissioner Rogers, formerly of Scotland Yard, is Security Chief, and Mr Barnes is a Crown Servant answerable directly to the Secretary of State for the Environment.'

'Well,' said Hugo, 'I am very flattered to have had a conducted tour and a free lunch from the top brass.'

'Our pleasure,' smiled Fallon, 'and you are probably wondering why the "top brass" has taken such a personal interest in your welfare, when we are very busy men with lots of problems.' He paused and leaned forward. 'Well, I'm afraid that one of those problems has become your good self! So we thought it best to invite you here and put one or two of our cards on the table.'

'Fair enough,' said Hugo. 'I shall cease to be one of your

problems when I know that my wife is safe and well.'

A flicker of impatience, and Fallon went on.

'Normally, Dr Brill, we are not in the least concerned with the capricious behaviour of errant wives or inflammatory journalists, unless some open breach of security is involved. In this case, because your concern for your wife is leading you to take steps, however pointless, that may cause us some degree of harassment, we have already instituted a search for Mrs Brill.' He leaned back and grimaced, staring at the desk. 'And I hope that if and when we find her the results will not prove too harassing for you!'

Hugo controlled himself. 'I happen to know that my wife is faithful, Major Fallon,' he said, 'and unless you have some evidence that she is an errant wife, I think your inference is pretty bad form!'

'Oh, come on, old boy!' Fallon thumped his fist on the desk. 'Why did you come up here before you knew she'd left? Why did you keep asking the staff who she was *with*? Hm?'

Hugo said nothing. These boys certainly did their homework.

'Your wife comes here,' continued Fallon, 'and openly admits she represents some nasty little muck-raking Trotskyist magazine, openly states in public places that she would stop at nothing to smother the Windscale project at birth! And still we let her make all her inquiries, see everything she wants to see! Why? Because we have nothing to hide!' He looked sharply to Barnes for support. 'We can stomach all the slurs and sneers that a trouble-making rag cares to print because nobody with any sense reads the bloody thing. But you, sir, are a different kettle of fish. Your wife has not kept you informed of her movements, so you behave like the worst kind of amateur detective. Good heavens, if she'd been up here trying to rouse public opinion against the use of toxic fertilisers, you

80

would probably have got your teeth into ICI! Or accused the local Farmer's Union of criminal abduction and made yourself a complete public idiot! But instead, you are trying to discredit us, and that is a much more serious matter.'

He paused to let this sink in, and Hugo realised that his two straight lefts to the beer belly in the Cold Pike Hotel had hit home harder than he could ever have imagined.

'The new Windscale project has already taken a severe panning from the National press,' went on Fallon vehemently, 'but believe me, Dr Brill, we are sailing full ahead for the Plutonium Economy! Unless, of course, you want to see the free nations of the world held to ransom by a bunch of Arab buccaneers! They can't smash Israel by force, so they are turning the screws – call it pure bloody avarice, or a stroke of political genius – on the friends of Israel! In a word, unless you want to see us brought to our knees, then taken over by the Commies or the National Front within this decade, you must see that we have to become independent of external sources of energy! Windscale must go ahead, the nuclear power programme must be protected – at any cost! And I mean *any* cost!'

David Niven had really left the scene. This was Boris Karloff, polishing up his thumb screws and opening the door to the Iron Maiden. Hugo puffed out his cheeks and expelled a long sigh.

'Major Fallon,' he said, 'I understand very well what you are saying. I understand that we are in a state of emergency. I understand that the Government is also in a state of panic, sufficient to push them ahead with the nukes, with too little concern for the broader philosophical issue of a species that is tampering with the bio-chemical basis of its very existence. That die is cast, as you say, whatever the cost! But, damn it all, my wife is missing, and I have this overwhelming conviction, right here in my bones, that

81

she is still up here! And, so help me, I think you know where she is!'

Fallon let out a short, harsh laugh, and leaned back in his chair. Jack Pallance unfolded his arms for a moment and stood erect – then slowly folded them again and leaned back against the wall. But Barnes was looking down at the table. And his eyes were clouded with concern, and something like embarrassment. He isn't one of them, thought Hugo, this isn't his line of work. He is a civil servant, doing his job. The other two are professional killers!

Barnes looked at the other two for a moment, then leaned forward.

'Dr Brill,' he said. 'We have really gone to a great deal of trouble to relieve your anxieties about your wife. Your best course is to go home and wait for her to return or contact you, as I am sure she will. But there is no justification, however much you are under stress, for you to repay our efforts with such an irresponsible accusation.'

'Now be fair,' said Hugo. 'I was lured here with a message that you may have news of my wife!'

'Hardly lured,' said Barnes, 'and the news is that we have instigated a search for her, and we hope you will be patient and accept our help.'

Hugo looked at the three men carefully, wondered if he should play them along, promise to be good, then go back to London and kick up hell. But suddenly he couldn't face the suspense of the journey back. His stomach ached with anguish for Jenny, his mind was filled with fragments of doubt, the disconnected minutiae that were pressing for cohesive explanation. And if there was one that linked Jenny with Windscale, then these men, whatever game they were playing, could have it for him now.

'I may be over-reacting under stress, Mr Barnes, and if I am wrong and my wife is safe, then I apologise. But if she is in any kind of trouble, any kind of danger, then I want to share it with her.' Fallon dropped his elbows on the desk, cupping his chin in his hands. Barnes arched his head back, but kept his eyes on Hugo. 'You see, I have not been behaving like the worst kind of amateur detective. I am – with all humility in the presence of professionals – a trained observer. I am a social anthropologist, a scientist who submits himself to the arbitration of observable facts.' Fallon groaned and leaned back in his seat, arms folded, and stared blankly at Hugo. 'No, Major Fallon, I have not been playing detective. I have been the victim of my own habits of perception, noting trivia that didn't fit normal patterns, body language inconsistent with personality.'

And Hugo began to give them an account of all the little things that had been happening to him, from the moment he had arrived at the Cold Pike Hotel the previous evening, all barely within the space of twenty hours. As he spoke, he found himself observing the reactions of the three men, looking carefully at their eyes as he dropped in each one of his observations, slowly outlined the working hypothesis that had given them some kind of meaning.

Barnes was looking at him with growing sympathy and open respect. Fallon's eyes had lost their hostility and were calculating, appraising, identifying with his own techniques. Even Jack Pallance, shifting his weight from leg to leg, showed a flicker of interest.

The sliver of soap was a winner; the shifted briefcase made Fallon's eye twitch, almost imperceptibly, towards Pallance; the contradiction over the suitcase brought Pallance's eye twitching less imperceptibly towards Fallon; the description of Barnes's evasive body language brought a twitch into both sets of eyes; the mosaic of office cells made it in three; and Jenny's cigarette scooped the pool with three changes of body posture. Hugo had no idea how deep he was getting in, but he felt an inordinate sense of relief as he got the niggling little devils off his chest and dropped them on to theirs.

'In the Cold Pike Hotel,' he said to Fallon, 'you reacted strongly to my inquiry about the County police. I deliberately mentioned Scotland Yard and my contacts at the Ministry and you didn't even finish your beer. In no time at all I am heisted back here, and brought, in a security lift, into the presence of three men who have previously assumed different public identities. Something was important enough to make you blow your cover. And for all your assertions that you have nothing to hide, you have gone to considerable lengths to let me see that you *have*, and then to persuade me to go home and shut up and wait.'

Fallon seemed about to speak but Barnes silenced him with the merest turn of a head.

'Yes, before you discount every damned insignificant thing that I have said, and tell me that I haven't an iota of proof, as if I didn't know it already, I must just say this. Half of these facts, plus your exhaustive knowledge of my intentions, point to a security surveillance on me from the moment I arrived. I am not going to quote you Chapter Seven of the Parker Report, or complain about inroads on my civil liberties, but that kind of surveillance suggests the extension of a previous surveillance on my over-zealous wife. And since the other half of the facts suggest that Jenny was brought here in exactly the same way that I was, and her bag was packed by Jack – er – Commissioner Rogers after she left at twelve o'clock, and that Major Fallon was on hand to cover up the possible abduction, I think my irresponsible accusation is possibly somewhere near to the responsible truth!'

There was a deep silence for a few moments. Hugo waited, dreading the attack, the annihilation of his thesis; he looked at the men, found himself taking deep breaths to slow his thumping heart.

'For God's sake!' he suddenly burst out, 'if she is in any

trouble, involve me! If you've shot her, shoot me too! But please – I beg you – tell me where she is!'

He realised he was near to tears and arched his head upwards and closed his eyes. He heard the noise of chairs scraping back and forced himself to look. Barnes and Fallon were on their feet, the big man was standing to attention, watchful, behind them.

'Dr Brill, will you excuse us for a few moments? Rogers!' The muscle nodded and stood back to let them pass. The door opened and closed, and Hugo heard their footsteps dying away along the concrete floor. Jack Pallance moved across and offered Hugo a cigarette. He lit it, and smoked it all the way down, his mind a complete blank, his body relaxed, numb, nerveless, still.

Even when the door opened behind him he didn't turn, didn't move as Barnes and Fallon came back behind the desk.

'Well, old boy, be it on your own head!' It was Fallon speaking, no, by heaven, David Niven was back, the eyes were suddenly crinkling, the man was human again. 'We have been authorised, in view of the special circumstances, to put you in the picture. You are to be involved, God help you, you are to be dropped right in it up to your anthropological neck!'

Barnes gave a shrug, motioned Fallon to be serious. Jack Pallance stood behind them, his eyes flicking quickly from one to the other. Wait a minute! Barnes! Of course! He looked like – like Claude Rains! Yes! The whole thing was an old Hollywood film, there had to be a happy ending! Fallon spoke again.

'Your powers of deduction are pretty good, Dr Brill, you barely missed a trick. And as for you, Rogers, next time you turn a place over, check the bloody squares on the coverlet!'

Pallance folded his arms, closed his eyes. The others

chuckled. Hugo couldn't. He couldn't believe this was happening. He had been prepared to give up and go home. Somehow he had got through and it was too much.

'However,' continued Fallon, 'nothing that you have told us would mean a brass farthing to anyone outside this room. We do not have to tell you a thing!'

'No, Dr Brill,' said Barnes, 'we are going to break security and involve you in a very serious affair, for our own reasons. And the price you will have to pay is your absolute and unconditional silence – and, I am afraid, your peace of mind. Now that I have said this to you, there is no way back!'

'You have my word,' said Hugo. His mouth was dry, crackled as he spoke. 'And I will have no peace of mind, in any case, until I get Jenny back.'

'Well,' said Fallon, 'let's see what we can do.' He reached out his hand, and Barnes gave him a large file that he had been carrying under his arm. Fallon opened it with a shrug of resignation, took a deep breath. 'This is the unpublished official Report on the Windscale Fire of 1957. Let me give you some idea what happened.' He began to speak, barely referring to the file, putting it into his own words.

'The first large-scale reactors built after the second World War were designed solely to produce plutonium for nuclear weapons. Unlike the Calder Hall reactor which you inspected this morning, the plutonium production reactor was, quite simply, a cube of graphite, perforated, end to end, with horizontal, not vertical channels. Rather like the racks in a wine cellar. Except they didn't lay down claret, they inserted cylindrical slugs of uranium-238 clad in aluminium, a very heady wine.'

With quite a hangover, thought Hugo, but he didn't say it.

'The fuel slugs were irradiated, then pushed through the graphite channels into a tank of water and processed into plutonium-239 and other fission products. Now. The first two British plutonium production reactors were opened here in 1952, on the site of a disused ordnance factory. It was christened Windscale, and you are now underneath it!'

It's a change from being on top, thought Hugo.

'The reactors were cooled by air, blown through the graphite channels and discharged through the 126-metre plant stacks, which you may have noticed.'

'May have noticed?' Hugo raised his eyebrows. 'The lighthouses with the knobs on top?'

'Ha! How apt!' smiled Fallon, and Barnes nodded grimly. 'Lighthouses indeed, warning of dangers in the darkness. And the "knobs" on top are filters, Dr Brill, designed to trap radiation within the plant stack. Sir John Cockroft designed them and insisted on having them fitted as a necessary precaution. His opponents called them "Cockroft's Folly" and that, as you will see, is precisely what they proved to be.'

'I don't understand,' said Hugo. 'I gather that during the fire, the filters reduced a national catastrophe to the level of a joke on the Milk Marketing Board. I see no folly in precaution.'

'No folly in precaution, but oh, my God, Dr Brill, folly in effect!'

Barnes shook his head. 'No, Major,' he insisted. 'I prefer to call it "Cockroft's Miracle"!'

'As you please,' said Fallon. 'However. On the 8th of October, 1957, as will happen in the best-run houses, the technician in charge of Windscale Number One read his meter wrongly. His instruments told him that the core temperature was falling so he gave it a boost. Fair enough. But his instruments didn't tell him that they were not connected to the hottest part of the core. Yes, he should have known that but he didn't. So he gave it another boost for luck. This time, his meter told him he had set the levels right. But the meter did not tell him that he had very quietly and unwittingly turned the heat up too far and set the core alight!'

Hugo remembered his apprehension in the control room at Calder Hall, the lone figure at the console, the question he had asked himself ever since – who was watching the man who was watching the wall?

'It can't happen at Calder Hall,' smiled Barnes, seeing the look in Hugo's eyes. 'Too many fail-safe precautions now, we have learnt many lessons in twenty-one years.'

'Yes,' said Fallon, impatient to continue. 'Anyway, those modest little meters kept their secret for two whole days. Then they registered that radioactivity was reaching the filters on the plant stacks. The balloon went up! But by this time, the graphite core was a raging inferno.' He paused. 'I will try to give you some idea of the dangers that now threatened not merely the Windscale plant, but all the northern counties of England, the Irish Sea, the Isle of Man, and possibly the whole of Ireland! It wasn't merely that eleven tonnes of molten uranium and everything else, including the graphite, were ablaze; it was that the air, far from cooling the blazing core, was shooting the flames through the hundred and fifty fuel channels and out of the discharge face like a monstrous bloody blow torch, playing on the concrete shielding of the reactor wall! And if that wall were to collapse through the intense heat, six hundred rem of lethal radiation would blast through and kill every living thing inside the reactor building! Office and admin. staff were evacuated immediately, a group of visiting students – physicists from Birmingham University – was sent packing, only a handful of expert technicians was allowed to stay and fight the blaze.' Fallon turned the pages of the file and looked closely at the contents. 'And that is not all . . . at the same time a state of emergency was notified to the Chief Constable of

Cumberland. Because someone had realised that there might also be an explosion of hydrogen mixed with air! And that would not only shatter the concrete shielding, but the *outer* wall as well. Goodbye Cumbria!'

Fallon stroked his forehead with the back of his hand and looked at Barnes. He picked up the report and waved it casually at Hugo.

'Now, Dr Brill, we come to the point where this official statement diverges from what actually happened. Here, you may read that the flames were finally subdued by bringing in the local Fire Brigade to pour water through the channels. The media were allowed to know that the only danger left was the cloud of radio-isotopes that had been released via the plant stacks. "Cockroft's Folly" trapped most of it inside the reactor, only iodine-131 was released into the atmosphere.'

'And they actually did pour the milk into the sea?'

'Oh, yes, they did indeed. A spectacular gesture to distract the Press and the public, a deliberately ludicrous piece of red tape, to keep the Windscale secret – what *really* happened – intact!'

He slapped the file contemptuously on to the desk and stared at it for a few moments.

'You have my undivided attention,' said Hugo, forgetting why he was there. 'What really happened at the Windscale fire?'

'Well,' continued Fallon at last, 'they did bring in the Fire Brigade. They did couple their hoses to the entry ports on the fuel channels and pour water through. The local Fire Chief, Roberts, and seven firemen, were in there with John Garland, a senior physicist, and his personal assistant, Mary Gregory, who refused to leave his side when he ordered everyone else out and dropped the seals on all the exits and windows. It was Friday, 11th October, 1957, at 8.55 a.m., when they turned on the firehoses. It

89

was at that moment that six of the student physicists from Birmingham University, three of them girls of eighteen, climbed out from the upper fuel-loading gantry where they had been hiding, determined to observe the outcome of the whole blasted cataclysmic affair! It was at that moment that these sixteen people, four of them young women, all taking their lives in their hands because they were heroes or idiots or – tchah! – pioneers of the nuclear age, were inside the Windscale No. 1 Plutonium Production Reactor building!'

He paused and closed his eyes.

'It was at that moment, Dr Brill, that the concrete shielding on the discharge face of the core blasted wide open and let loose the clouds of hell upon those sixteen human beings inside!'

There was silence for a long moment.

'My God,' breathed Hugo, 'I'm not surprised the Government wanted it all buttoned up. Did they recover the bodies? Or did they –?' He stopped and looked hard at the three men, looked at them one by one. 'Or did they just entomb them in concrete with the rest of it?'

'No, Dr Brill, they did not recover the bodies. But then, they didn't fill the reactors with concrete. They didn't do anything except seal off the entire plant with a double steel and concrete housing – because they wanted to keep the contents intact.'

'Well, that is a pretty gruesome national monument, Major Fallon, Sixteen corpses, preserved in a cloud of radioactive dust!'

'Not quite, Dr Brill,' said Fallon, his eyes hard and bright. 'You see – inside the Windscale No. 1 Plutonium Production building – inside your egg with its double steel and concrete shell and its mosaic of office buildings, its camouflage of normality – inside all that . . . they are all . . . still . . . very much . . . *alive*!'

PART 2

'On the shore of the wide world,
I stand alone . . .'

Chapter Nine

'Hello, Huggy love!'
The 'phone exploded at the other end.

'Jenny! Jenny, how are you? Where are you, are you home already?'

'No, Huggy, I'm still here.'

There was a moment's silence. Oh heck, she thought, you're going to be upset; please Hugo, please understand!

'Still there? Up there – in Cumberland? When will you be home? It's eleven-thirty now, when are you leaving?'

'I'm staying on darling, just a few days more. . . . I have to . . . I can't explain now but the story is more than I'd hoped.'

'What story? Are they still roasting the robins on Filingdale Moor? Don't say it, I made a bad joke. Jenny, why don't you come back today, go up again later? Where are you?'

Come back today, oh, Huggy darling, if only I could, she wanted to say, if only I could be there with you and hold you close and be safe and secure in your arms away

92

from this place, and think it all out and tell you what I have to do. But she couldn't say it and she knew she had to do it alone.

'Dear Huggy, don't make it difficult, I have to stay.'

There was no other way. She had put herself out on a limb, deliberately drawn attention to herself, made herself a target. By herself, she might draw their fire, bring them out into the open, crack the insidious wall of silence and smooth assurances that she had met with at every turn. And now at last, she was on to something. Alone, she might find it. Huggy mustn't be involved.

'Hey, wait a minute. You still at the Cold Pike Hotel? Look, I'll take a few days off, and come up and see you. I don't –'

'No!' Oh, heck, she shouldn't have said it like that. But he mustn't come, mustn't be involved. Not now. 'No, dear old Huggy, no . . . it's . . . it's easier if I do it alone. . . . I'm all over the place.'

There was no answer from him. No answer, she knew, because he was wondering why she had been so final, wondering why she didn't want him there, wondering – who she was with. That damned summer of '75 was always in his mind, always between them, the one flaw in their perfect love that she had never ceased to regret. And it was her fault. The search for an ideal beyond what she had found in Hugo, the search for a purity of heart, a transcendent mind and spirit beyond any ordinary human experience. The guru journalist had promised all this in his serene smile and wise young eyes and tranquil face. They had spent those days together in spiritual communion, with no physical contact, only an understanding and a soaring love for each other and the universe that enveloped them. Until she realised that the serene smile and the wise eyes were without substance, the peace he had found was his escape from involvement, her guru was just another

93

human being, rationalising inactivity into an ideal. It was a dream, and Hugo was real and she went back to him. But from that moment, he had known that she was seeking something beyond him, and was never secure with her again.

'It won't be long.' She ached to reassure him. 'I do miss you, darling, I miss you so much.'

'I love you, Jenny.'

'I love you, Huggy – oh, Jesus, look at the time, I must go. I'll be home in a couple of days, I promise. 'Bye, darling.'

''Bye, Jenny.'

She didn't hang up. He sounded like a small, lost boy. She pictured him there in his study, the ramshackle bookcase on the far wall, the desk facing the blackboard, the photos of Malinowski as a young man with the Kaiser moustache, the ethnic posters from the British Museum, his dear old, simple, cosy, academic retreat, where she had first been alone with him. All the memories of the marvellous days they had spent there together. Warm, secure, safe. Creeping into his room before the secretaries came to work, putting the solitary, red rose in his vase, the secret link with the man she had loved from the moment she saw him. Oh, to be there now, warm, secure, safe. Away from this nightmare that she had brought on herself and could not dream away. It was all she could do to speak again, her voice was tiny, small.

'Look after yourself, love.'

She hung up and leaned against the wall of the booth for a moment, eyes closed, filling with tears, alone. To be there with him now. Warm, secure, safe. She inhaled slowly, held her breath for a moment, huffed it out and snapped back into action. A trick she had learned from Hugo. Be positive, cast out grief and despondency, begone dull dread and woe, start working, just start, *start* it! Begin! *Do* it! The work itself is the panacea, the act itself is sufficient cause! She went up the stairs two at a time, along the corridor to room 27. Her dossier was out of her case and on to the chequered coverlet, and she sat on the bed, riffling through her notes.

She had been here for two weeks, dropped on Windscale and its work force like an avenging angel. She had notes on over a hundred interviews and four visits to Windscale. Visit one, to make the punter's tour of Calder Hall; visit two, to explore the AGR and the other out-buildings; visit three, to interview as many of the technicians as she could fit in; and visit four, to go round the old Windscale reactor-cum-office block. That was yesterday morning; Tuesday. Until that visit, she had been given the most charming and maddening runaround of her life. She had been allowed to see everything. She had found nothing. It was all so damned clean and free of pollution, everybody was so damned helpful, Mr Barnes was the model of civilised concern.

Until yesterday morning. Visit four! When she had found what she wanted! A disaster! A bloody great, covered-up, plutonium-239 disaster! The Windscale Fire! It was the morning that Mr Barnes had, all at once, lost a great deal of his charm. She had sped back to the Cold Pike in a frenzy of impatience, snatched a quick snack and a beer, and had a few words with that old smoothie, George Fallon, who spent so much time in the bar he should have hung his boards outside. How that idiot liked to lead her on, tease her about the 'revolution', would she elect him Commissar of Cumbria? But he was a mine of information about who lived where and did what, so she had swallowed his jibes and picked his brains, and actually quite liked the old pomp. She asked him where she could find the local fire station. He told her, with a transient look of concern that didn't quite fit his vacuous eyes. Who cared, let him think she was mad, she had made the leap from empirical fact to deductive theory, good old Hugo had taught her well. She had linked Windscale with Mrs Barratt and the puzzle of the cosy cottage in Gosforth.

'Thank you, George,' she had said, and pecked him on the head and gone upstairs to check through her dossier.

It was all there! In the interview with Jessie Barratt, Rose Cottage, Gosforth. One of the scores of interviews she had been carrying out in the surrounding villages, noting premature deaths, unexplained illnesses, sterility, cancer, any possible symptoms of the long-term effects of radiation poisoning, all to be checked against the national average. The locals were helpful, thought she was a bit odd. They didn't mind Windscale now, it was part of the scenery; it made a lot of work and it was a sight cleaner than those dreadful coal mines on the north coast.

She knew that her interviews were not really much use, had no scientific validity. But Jessie Barratt had stuck in her mind.

A small, wizened lady, aged sixty-four, widowed for twenty-one years. Her husband, a local fireman, had died in 1957 and was buried in the nearby churchyard. He hadn't been a fireman all his life; before that he was a farm labourer, then worked in a garage repairing cars and gone into the fire service soon after. He was forty-five when he died; it was a heart attack and nothing more, and he had left her a mite of money so she wasn't so badly off. That was what had puzzled Jenny.

Rose Cottage was beautiful. Even allowing for house prices twenty-one years ago, it was way beyond the means of a fireman's wife. She would have needed an inheritance or a win on the pools to buy such a place. And that wasn't all. Jessie Barratt moved and spoke with a serenity that was unusual even in an ageing woman. She had the air of somebody who had found an infinite peace of mind, the look of somebody who knew something very beautiful – and very secret. Jenny had adored her. And remembered. And made the connection. Wife of a fireman who died in 1957. Windscale Fire, 1957.

Back downstairs, into her hired Marina, nice sunny afternoon, pleasant drive to Gosforth, perfect day to wander in the local churchyard and think of Thomas Gray. 'Beneath those rugged elms, that yew tree's shade . . .' And that was where she found it. A simple tombstone: 'John Barratt, born March 9th, 1912, died October 11th, 1957, aged 45 years.' If October 11th was the date of the Windscale Fire, it was too much of a coincidence. If he had died in the fire, who else was with him? And was it released to the papers? And why didn't Jessie Barratt mention it?

Into the car, round the winding lanes again, back to Seascale. The local Fire Station was easy to find, the little man in the office very helpful, pulled out the dusty old staff records. 1957 was missing! Suspicious! Excellent! Especially since 1956 recorded John Barratt, then of The Lanes, Seascale, and five other men. And 1958 recorded none of them. Jenny took their names and addresses and spent the rest of the day checking them out. Four of them had moved away from the area. One – Adam Williams of Calderbridge – had died – in 1957!

The day was used up, Jenny was tired out. She went back to the Cold Pike for a bath and a huge dinner. In bed later, she couldn't sleep. Her mind was too active, her stomach was filled with food and wine, dyspepsia and disquiet. Why was she so nervous? Excitement? Fear? Bad vibrations? Or the faintest shadow of a suspicion that everything she did – was being observed! That she was baiting a trap – with herself!

Tomorrow, she had to check the relatives of the man who had died in 1957. Check with the local registrars in all the villages from Egremont to Drigg, for everyone who had died in that year. And visit Jessie Barratt once more and

97

ask her a lot of very loaded questions. Because tomorrow, she had to find out what had happened at Windscale in 1957!

Well, the day was here, now. She had got up late, over-slept after her restless night. Got up late, not wanting to face the day. Got up, not wanting to do the things she had to do. But she had called Jeremy at *Change!* and set the machinery in motion – asked for everything he could find out about the '57 Fire. She had called Hugo to tell him she needed a few more days, and stirred up emotions buried in the excitement of the search. Blast! Why didn't she just go back to London now, reassure him and give herself a break? No! A day or so, and she'd have the facts she needed. Then back to London and let loose the dogs of war!

She put the dossier in her airline bag, with plenty of spare notepaper and pencils, and went downstairs. Just time for a quick Guinness at the bar, a brief chat with the busty Swede and she was ready.

It was twelve o'clock. Her Marina was parked near the portico. As she went to get it, she noticed that a black Cortina was parked a few yards away. There were two men inside. As she opened her door, one of the men climbed out and walked across to her.

'Mrs Brill?'

'Yes?'

'I have a message from Mr Barnes at Windscale. He says he would like to see you in his office.'

'How nice. I'm afraid I have some rather urgent business now, but perhaps I can call on him later when I'm passing.'

'Well, I'm afraid he can only see you now. Oh, and he did say that he has turned up some facts that will save you a great deal of time.'

The man waited patiently, insistently for her answer. There was something in his manner that suggested she had no alternative. If she refused, would they take her by force?

Just what she wanted! Two men sent to bring her in! Marvellous! But, for the moment, play it cool.

'Oh, well, in that case I'll follow you over.'

'Er – we have clearance at the gate, we can take you straight to him and bring you back.'

'How nice of you,' said Jenny and walked over to the Cortina. The other man climbed out to let her in, closed the door and walked into the hotel. Jenny didn't say a word. It was all so nice and suspicious, the first time anything had happened out of key with the maddening normality that had almost persuaded her that she was wasting her time. What was waiting for her at Windscale? Threats? Force? Then she would know they had something to hide. Oh, come on, darling Hugo, how's that for woman's intuition?

Mr Barnes was waiting at the entrance to the old block; he hurried to greet her warmly and usher her into his office, a few yards from an elevator and a waiting-room. He offered her some coffee and showed her the unpublished Official Report on the Windscale Fire in 1957. She read it through very carefully, very quietly, everything from the first idiotic blunder to the victory of the fire hoses, the sequel of the sour milk in the sea, the lengthy reassurances that no other ill effects had occurred or were likely to occur in the future. Jenny read parts of it over again, then sat with it on her knee, looking at the cover. The date of the fire was October 11th, 1957. The date on John Barratt's tombstone.

'There you are, Mrs Brill,' said Barnes cheerfully, 'that is the full official report on the fire. It's all there. I'll be absolutely frank with you, you write for the kind of magazine that I abhor, and you want us closed down –'

'We print nothing but the truth,' said Jenny.

'The truth?' smiled Barnes. 'Well, sometimes that is just a pretty name for bigotry. Anyway. You want us closed

99

down. Fair enough. You can waste your time making inquiries and you can try to stir up that old disaster as much as you like. But it will do you no more good than if you were to protest against the first failures in the history of aviation. It's still the only way to travel.'

'And we still have plane crashes,' said Jenny. 'You had no moral right to gamble with survival in the '50s, you have no right now!'

Barnes nodded. 'It was a dreadful gamble in those days. But give us some credit, we have learnt from our mistakes. We don't *seek* disasters! We now have triple fail-safe systems and sophisticated monitoring that makes any recurrence of that blunder impossible.' Jenny said nothing. 'Well, Mrs Brill, are you satisfied now?'

'Oh, yes, Mr Barnes,' said Jenny, and looked him directly in the eye. 'I think I've got it.'

'Good,' said Barnes, rising abruptly. 'Well, must press on! I'll have the car over to take you back to your hotel. Will you be leaving for London today?'

'No,' smiled Jenny, 'I'm going to check all the local registrars of births and deaths. I want to find out who died around here on October 11th, 1957!'

Barnes was smooth. Oh, he was so smooth. He didn't even flicker an eyelid. He just kept moving and ushered her out of his office, indicated the waiting room in the main hall.

'If you will wait here, Mrs Brill?'

Jenny sat down on one of the chairs and lit a Benson and Hedges tipped, puffed it a few times and stubbed it out in the sand tray. 'Sorry, Hugo,' she murmured, 'it *is* an ugly habit.' She pushed the bent stub out of sight and idly smoothed the sand across it. She had a sudden awful sense of defeat. Barnes was right. The Windscale Fire was ancient history, nobody would give a damn. And her two dead firemen didn't seem such a brilliant find now. Even if they had both died on the same date, even if they had both died in the fire, Barnes was still right. The tragedy was long over, covered up or not; the conspirators were all retired or dead, it couldn't harm the nukes now. It would be like exposing Watergate twenty-one years after Nixon had left office. Barnes had quietly called her bluff, explained her away, smoothed the sand over her bad habits and fiery protests.

The door opened and the driver appeared.

'Mrs Brill, this way please.'

Jenny followed him aimlessly. Might as well give up and go home and cry it all out on Hugo's shoulder. She hardly noticed that they had stopped at the door of a lift. Then the man turned a key in the lock and the doors opened. Jenny followed him at once, her spirits rising. All good cloak and dagger stuff! The lift went down. Oh, heck, it's only going to be an underground garage!

But it wasn't. It was going to be a small room along a concrete corridor, with Fallon's partner, Rogers, and George himself, both sitting at a desk looking very stern. Jenny's heart pounded and leapt! *Them?* Here? They were in it! And they had shown their hand at last! Why? *Why?*

'I do *not* believe it,' she said. 'What are you doing here, George?'

'Mrs Brill,' said Fallon, 'I am Major Fallon and this is Commander Rogers. We are security officers and you are being a very naughty girl!'

'Yes, George,' smiled Jenny, 'and you have blown your cover. Now why, in heaven's name, would you do that for a tacky little time-wasting journalist like me?'

'I'm afraid it's a little more serious than you imagine, Mrs Brill. You will not be allowed to report this meeting, nor anything that is said here, and you will kindly answer my questions.'

'I do not have to answer any questions, George.'

'Then we will keep you here until you do.'

Jenny was silent.

'Now, Madam, do you consider yourself a revolutionary?'

They were looking at her, cold-eyed, Rogers's pen poised over a file of papers. Jenny pursed her lips in surprise.

'Well, then, that is a question I might like to discuss. Yes, I do. Insofar as I believe in radical changes in the social and economic structure of a country, particularly to prevent the exploitation of dangerous resources in the interests of commercial profit.'

'And do you believe these changes should be brought about by armed insurrection or violence?'

'Well, you really know how to hurt a girl, George. It all depends, doesn't it! If this were a Fascist country there would be no alternative. In a moderately effective democracy, we can achieve a great deal by publishing the truth, awakening the electorate to the dangers, forming pressure groups, canvassing MPs, and . . .' she paused significantly, 'resisting any attempts to deny us that freedom.'

'Do you take narcotics?'

'Do I *what*?'

'Answer the question!'

'Don't talk bloody rot! I hate narcotics!'

'Have you any affiliations with the Worker's Revolutionary Party?'

'No, I am not a Trot and I don't believe in permanent revolution!'

'The IRA?'

'Now listen, Mr Fallon, this nonsense has gone far enough. I have nothing to do with the Red Brigade, the PLO or Yasser Arafat. I am not a terrorist, I line up with Friends of the Earth, the Council for the Protection of Rural England, the National Council for Civil Liberties and Spike Milligan!'

'And in so doing, you play into the hands of the disruptive forces and the extremists, whose only aim is to destroy the social fabric of this country, undermine

102

authority, and foster anarchy and chaos.'

'What sort of an imbecile do you – ?'

'You are extremely naïve, Mrs Brill, if you think that your mulish efforts to discredit the nuclear power programme can do anything but harm!' He seemed to soften a little, changed his tack. 'You must see that Britain needs energy as the body needs blood.'

'And bad blood kills.'

Fallon stood up and slammed his fist hard on the table.

'Mrs Brill, why the hell don't you just give up and go home!'

If only you knew, George, she thought, I had been about to do just that. But not now!

Fallon paced angrily around the room. 'Why don't you apply all your considerable brains and dedication to the preservation of wild life, saving the seals, sorting out juvenile delinquents. . . .'

'I do that too,' said Jenny.

Fallon moved across to her, put his face close, shaking his head like a kindly uncle.

'You're an attractive girl, happily married, why don't you settle down and nurse a few babies?'

'I think that the survival of the entire human species is a much worthier cause, Mr Fallon. The Luddites fought the Industrial Revolution and failed. But I have yet to be convinced that they were wrong.'

'Well, you won't find many people –'

'And now we are all slithering down the slope into the Plutonium Age and I don't think that you or the scientists or anyone else on the helter-skelter has any idea what is waiting at the bottom.'

Fallon gave a wry smile, and exchanged a look with Rogers. He nodded slowly, as if he were laughing at some private joke, and sat down again. 'As I was about to say, Mrs Brill, you won't find many people who share your

103

desire to go back to the land. We live in a rather different world in which I have a job to do. And that is the surveillance and prevention of subversive, violent or unlawful activities, towards which you are fast moving perilously close.'

'Yes,' said Jenny, fumbling angrily in her bag for her notes, not caring too much if they confiscated the lot. It was all useless, anyway, she knew she was beaten, but the man was beginning to infuriate her with his threats and innuendoes.

'Let me quote you from the Sixth Report of the Royal Commission on Environmental Pollution. Here! "The unquantifiable effects of the security measures that might become necessary in a plutonium economy, should be a major consideration in decisions on substantial nuclear development." In other words, Mr Fallon, you people only have to go a bit too far and you'll put the stopper on the whole damned thing yourselves!'

'When we go too far,' said Fallon slowly, with a chilling look that reminded her where she was, 'we make sure that nobody knows about it.' There was silence for a moment, then, with a hint of concern in his voice, 'Mrs Brill, this has become distasteful and embarrassing. I am now satisfied that your intentions are not subversive but misguided. Will you please go home and allow us to do our job?'

'I will go home,' said Jenny, 'when I have completed my legitimate and lawful investigations. That is *my* job. I am paid to do it and I am legally entitled to do it. For heaven's sake, if you are right, what have you to worry about?'

Fallon looked at Rogers helplessly. 'But what are you looking for? What do you expect to find?'

'I want to know,' said Jenny, with a sudden reckless determination to test her intuition on them, once and for all, 'who died or disappeared in this area in October, 1957. I have a feeling that some of them may have died in the

Windscale Fire and it was all hushed up. And I want to know why. But more than that . . . I want to know why the relatives didn't make a fuss. Why someone like Jessie Barratt, for example, is living in a house beyond her means.'

Fallon didn't move. Rogers put his pen back in his pocket and closed his folder. They made no attempt to discredit her remarks as Barnes had done with so much skill. Jenny found herself staring at them, let herself sink back in the chair. She went on, not knowing why, just testing . . . testing . . .

'Yes, more than anything,' she said, 'before I go home, I want to talk, just once more, to Jessie Barratt.'

Chapter Ten

The room was silent as the tomb. Nobody moved, nobody spoke. Jenny was astounded. She had said no more to them than she had to Barnes. Except to mention Jessie Barratt. But why were they reacting like this? No questions, no threats. It was as if they had suddenly cut themselves off from all contact with her, ceased, in that instant, even to acknowledge her existence.

Then Fallon was on his feet and nodding to Rogers to follow him. He stopped at the door and half turned his head, still not looking at her.

'Will you please wait here, Mrs Brill?' He seemed about to say more, then tightened his lips. The door clicked behind them and their footsteps echoed away down the corridor.

Jenny stood up and realised that her knees were not supporting her too well. The coldness of the two men was suddenly frightening. She realised she was here alone, up against a law outside the law, the ruthless domain of the secret police. She had no idea what they would do, how far they would go. But she had wanted something like this to happen, so she must just bloody well hang in there and see it through. She tried the door to see if they had locked her in. They had not. Curious. She opened the door and peered out. Nobody in sight. Nobody on guard. Curiouser and curiouser.

Then all at once she was filled with a fierce and feminist indignation, furious that they had brought her here, interrogated her like a criminal, intruded upon her civil liberties. In going that step too far they had finally given her what she needed. The plutonium economy must, on these terms, presuppose the police state. Because it was happening now, to her! She must get out and get it into print. But they would surely have realised this when they showed their hand. If there was no way to silence her, how could they let her out? What were they deciding now, and at what level? And how *dare* they!

Jenny Brill was going to make a run for it! She was going to get back to London, then Jeremy would make it all so unbelievably public that they would not dare arrest her for fear of aggravating the scandal.

She tiptoed fast as she could along the corridor until it turned sharp left and passed a heavy iron grill covering a steel door. She slowed and ducked low, in case there was a peep-hole, and hurried on. Then, all at once, she became aware that the light was increasing ahead. She hugged the wall of the corridor and saw that, about fifty feet on, it crossed a bright open space and continued on the other side.

She crept closer, suddenly noticed that a pair of parallel metal tracks ran across the opening. And a low humming noise, like a turbine or a diesel engine, was steadily increasing in volume. Then, almost at the opening, she stifled a scream and shot back some twenty feet to press herself flat against the wall!

A huge, metal bulk, shaped like a railway container, appeared from the right, moving very slowly across the intersection. It was about twenty feet long, made of aluminium or steel, painted with wide, black, diagonal stripes, and moving without human agency: a cybernetic delivery truck or a robot railway under remote control. As it disappeared, Jenny flitted again to the corner, peeped right and left. Nobody about. She ventured out onto the track, kept her feet clear of the rails in case they were electrified. The back of the container was open, filled with sacks and boxes and metal drums. She followed it up and looked in. Incredible! The sacks were marked: 'Corn', 'Soya', 'Rice'; the boxes were stamped: 'Unrefined Barbados'; the drums: 'Maize Oil' and 'Sunflower Oil'. Ye gods! Health foods! Then she noticed that the container was steadily disappearing into the wall ahead, moving between latticed gates – into a lift! Hey, what goes down must come up, this was a way out. Unless it went down? She had no choice, it's all or nothing now, my girl! She climbed quickly up into the container and hid between the sacks of soya and rice.

The container stopped, the gates whirred across, the lift began to move – upwards! Thank God, she murmured, the secret health-food eaters live above the ground. It was pitch dark. She heard a hissing beneath her, then a thud, as if something had slid across to seal off the lift shaft. She heard it again, then again! Triple sealed? With what? And why? The lift stopped without a tremor, the truck was moving off it and gliding forward again into a dim light. Jenny stuck her nose around the corner of her soya sack and squinted for a moment, adjusting to the gloom.

She seemed to see a vast space, around and above her, like an aircraft hanger, with overhead pulleys and catwalks, a spider's web of steel girders, spun from wall to wall. And passing slowly by, like the crumbling ruins of Leptis

Magna, a tapestry of concrete blocks and wooden buildings and cylindrical vessels and – control panels.

Oh, my God, thought Jenny, I know where I am! No great tax upon the intellect to put this little two and two together, I am inside the old Windscale plant, inside the sealed-off building, the reactor's graveyard! For a brief instant, a panic seized her, a terrible dread that she was immersed in lethal, radioactive dust, plutonium-239 with a half-life of 24,000 years. But Barnes's report calmed her again. It said that the shielding had held, the reactor building was clean, the reactor entombed in concrete. She drew her hand across her brow. Where was this silver beetle taking her? Where was the way out?

Then all at once the beetle began to descend a slope. It was passing through an arch set in the far wall. As it came out the other side, she saw that the gloom was giving way to bright light, pure and fresh as a spring day. It seemed to come from a translucent ceiling high above; it couldn't be sunlight, surely, she was still below ground.

The first sub-tropical plant took her breath away. A Joshua tree, a majestic yucca, reaching up its spiky arms in supplication to heaven! Then another! And a magnolia tree? It couldn't be. But the scent was strong and the blooms were shaped like champagne glasses, bright and white and glowing. She was passing through a forest of succulent plants, the world of Henri Rousseau, lush, exotic vegetation that surely could never exist outside a painter's imagination.

Jenny's eyes were opened wide, the child she had always been had no thought now of danger; Fallon and nuclear fission were distant traces in her memory. She climbed to the tailboard of the beetle and dropped quietly on to the track.

And that was when she first heard the birdsong, muted but rich, thrilling musical sounds that reminded her of

Hugo's favourite poem:

> *'Listen Eugenia –*
> *Hark how the bursts come crowding through the leaves'.*

No thought of danger now, this was the child in wonderland. She walked into the beauty of the inviting flora, touched the petals and the leaves in awe. A sudden flurry of sound, from behind, had her leaping round in shock! But there was nothing there! Only the leaves swishing back into place! Who else was here? What else? A parrakeet swooped down onto a branch beside her, examined her with a beady eye and flew off. Birds! What else? Who else? And then, ahead, through the shining foliage, she saw the hut!

A simple, primitive building with thatched roof and adobe walls, orange walls covered with crude graffiti. No, wait! Look closer! They were superb, brightly coloured designs that reminded her of the prehistoric cave paintings she had seen, with Hugo, in Lascaux and the Dordogne, red, brown and yellow ochres and charcoal black. She wandered around the small building, entranced, marvelling at the simplicity of the primitive forms, wondering who did them, unable to believe this was all real and not a hallucination.

Then, above the birdsong, she distinguished another sound, a low crooning call that seemed to come from a hundred throats; dissonant, yet with the sweetness of a Gregorian chant; a plainsong of peace that might have come from the early Christians, chanting in sanctuary, the Catacombs of Rome. Was it a human sound, she wondered, or only the wind, whispering through the dead world that lay back there behind the arch?

She stopped and gasped! A figure was standing in the shadows, half-masked by the vegetation, watching her.

110

'Hello, who's there?' she cried out, her voice husky with alarm. 'Anybody there?'

She made a step towards it, and, in that same instant, the figure seemed to lurch at her, lumbering forward, huge, thickset, covered in some kind of shining, silken gloss! The light fell upon the monstrous head, the jutting upper jaw and the heavy, chinless jowl, the brutish nose, with its wide, flat bridge filling two-thirds of the massive brow, the eyes flickering like small red demons in the tiny sockets at each side!

And Jenny, her nerves taut, her imagination already heightened by the wonder and fear of all that was happening, found herself screaming and screaming in uncontrolled terror, screaming and falling and swooning into a dark and blessed oblivion.

Chapter Eleven

'Alive?'

'Alive.'

'After twenty-one years?'

'Twenty-one years.'

Hugo sat there, staring blankly at Fallon, boggling at the implications of this incredible statement. Then Barnes stood up sharply, collecting his papers together with an air of finality.

'Right!' he said, 'now you know, Dr Brill.' He looked at Fallon. 'Will you take him up?' Fallon nodded. 'Very well. Then I want you and Rogers to report immediately to my office!' He went out, slamming the door behind him.

Fallon sat glowering at the door for a moment, chewing the inside of his cheek, exchanged a quick look with Rogers, came round the desk and slapped Hugo on the shoulder. It was a hard slap and it hurt. Hugo looked up at him in surprise. What's griping him, he wondered.

'Come on, Doctor, in for a penny, in for a pound, now we hand you over to the boffins!'

Hugo was standing up, walking to the door, following Fallon and Rogers (no games now with film star names, these men were in deadly earnest); they were walking briskly along the concrete corridor, turning left, on a few feet, stopping in front of a heavy iron grill which covered a steel door. The loony-bin, thought Hugo, they're going to lock themselves up and take me with them!

Fallon pressed a small, plastic card into a slot.

'Who is it?' It was an intercom set in the wall.

'Fallon.'

The grill lifted and the door opened and they went in. Perhaps it was the contrast with the grey, deserted corridor that hit Hugo so hard. He hadn't had such a jolt since the time he went through the modest front door of No. 10 Downing Street, and found himself in an endless labyrinth of majestic staircases and mirrored ballrooms.

In this case, the small, steel door plunged him into a vast radio-chemical centre, sprawling with thermonuclear apparatus and something like a dozen separate laboratories, ranged in pairs for about five hundred feet to the right, and three hundred feet ahead. All this, and, once again, hardly a technician in sight. As Fallon led them between the laboratory blocks, Hugo could see that the whole complex was grouped around a massive construction in the centre. This was an older building than the rest, older than the glass-paned gallery that had been added to it, extending on all sides some twenty feet above the ground, like the base of a column.

'There are viewing ports in the control rooms,' said Fallon, with the air of a guide who was bored with the job, 'so the whole area of the old Windscale plant is under continuous surveillance.'

So that was it! The monolith was the base of the Windscale reactor building! And this scientific colony must have grown up around it in the last twenty-one years. Hugo put this to Fallon who nodded without much enthusiasm.

'They built all this underground from about 1959 onwards; and there is a great deal more on the other side. But Dr Kurnitz will give you a better idea of the crazy world you've just walked into. With your eyes wide open!'

They passed the last laboratory section and climbed a steel staircase set against the far wall. It led them up to a loft-like opening in the roof, where a guard let them through another steel door and grill. They were in a large building with windows. Windows! Letting in the sunshine and the sky, windows looking out on to Calder Hall and the cooling towers over to the east. Above ground again!

'I shall never more take anything for granted,' said Hugo to Fallon, 'it really is an amazing camouflage.'

Fallon grunted as if he liked his secrets kept but had no choice. He knocked on a door numbered '11' and went in, leaving Rogers standing guard, saying nothing.

Hugo had heard the name Kurnitz many years ago, just after the war. Kurnitz? Yes, he was the radio-biologist who had made definitive reports on the survivors of Nagasaki and Hiroshima. Abba Kurnitz, the biochemist from Berlin who had settled on an Israeli Kibbutz in 1936 to breed livestock. Now he was here in Cumberland.

Fallon came out and ushered Hugo into the presence, excused himself with a curt nod, and left with Rogers. Hm, thought Hugo, something smells in the state of Fallon! Just because I am out of his jurisdiction? For the time being? Odd fish!

Dr Kurnitz, now in his mid-sixties, was sitting behind a wide, cluttered desk, small, grey-haired, benign in his brown tweed suit and bow tie. He smiled at Hugo, indicated an armchair at his side.

'Well, Dr Brill, life plays many strange tricks, hm?'

'And always on me,' said Hugo.

Kurnitz chuckled. 'Now,' he said, carrying on as if his

meeting with Hugo were the most natural thing in the world, 'let me explain what has happened to date. I was consultant to the Atomic Bomb Casualty Commission after the war. The US sent me to Hiroshima and Nagasaki to supervise medical treatment and to document the effects of radiation on the survivors. Acute radiation injury, which shows up within days or weeks of exposure, will damage the red blood cells; higher dosage may affect the viscera and the central nervous system. The symptoms include nausea, vomiting, dizziness, aching eyes, itching skin, pigment changes and loss of appetite. The later consequences, liable to show up for years afterwards, even into old age, are leukaemia and other cancers, thyroid abnormalities, and genetic failure and mutation of offspring. In a word, wherever radiation shoots disruptive energy into living tissue, the symptoms should indicate the point of attack. All quite clear, codified and exhaustive. Or so I thought until I received an urgent call from the British Home Office in the November of 1957, three weeks after the fire. You have been told about that. The fire burnt itself out in two days, but the sixteen people inside were given up for lost. They could never have survived the 600 rem of radiation recorded inside the reactor building. A massive and complicated cover-up operation was mounted, but,' he shrugged, 'Major Fallon can tell you more about that.' Kurnitz said this with evident distaste. He doesn't like Fallon either, thought Hugo.

'Anyway, it was three weeks before a team, wearing double protective suiting, was allowed to begin decontamination. The first members of the team entered through the airlock, expecting to find a scene of devastation and death. It was not so. The reactor was destroyed. The rest of the interior was intact. They began to search for the bodies of the victims. There were none! Had there been total disintegration of all human tissue? What else could explain it? Then one of the searchers opened the door of the small canteen in the northern corner of the plant and gazed upon one of the most awesome sights of his life! Sixteen people were seated inside, eating a frugal meal, as if all the devastation and ionizing radiation around them had never happened! They were, miraculously, quite unharmed, no symptoms of radiation at all!

'One can only imagine the elation and relief that followed; the survivors must be taken out immediately for decontamination and hospitalization. But John Garland, the senior physicist and, inevitably, their natural leader, did not agree. They had survived three weeks in a lethal level of radiation. It was a miracle – or a freak – and required very careful handling. He would not let them leave without exhaustive tests. That was where I was called in. I agreed with Garland and I suggested that one volunteer from the irradiated group should come out for examination. If all was well with him, the rest would follow. Garland himself volunteered, insisted that with his expert knowledge he could better describe the subjective effect of the rehabilitation.

'He was decontaminated and moved to the medical block in great secrecy. For a day or two, he seemed to have made a complete recovery. No symptoms, his white blood cell count normal and constant. But on the third day he reported numbness in his fingers and severe internal pains. He fought against the delirium that followed but was soon incapable of any further observations that might assist us. I tugged at a lock of his hair and it came away. I ordered an immediate blood test and, as I expected, the white blood cell count had increased. Astounding! The other fifteen survivors were alive and well inside that radioactive environment, outside it, Garland was dying of undeniable radiation poisoning I could see no explanation in science for such a paradox, but made an immediate decision.

116

'On the wild hypothesis that he was dying outside his "natural" environment, as a fish dies out of water, I ordered him to be put back. Inside the reactor building, he immediately receovered!'

'Astounding, indeed!' murmured Hugo. 'The first Atomic Man.'

'You could say that, Dr Brill,' said Kurnitz, rising, 'but I suspect you would be wrong.' He walked over to gaze out of the window. 'We had been tampering with the unknown, without knowing.'

'My wife has been saying that for years, Dr Kurnitz.'

'Ah yes,' said Kurnitz, and turned to look at Hugo for a long moment. 'Your wife.' He lowered his eyes and looked at the floor, tugged at his bow tie a few times, murmured again, almost to himself: 'Your wife.' He pressed an intercom button and said 'Please send in Dr Benson.' Then he paced up and down in silence.

There was a tap at the door, and a young woman in her mid-thirties came in. She was neat and trim, with short blonde hair, and wearing a white house-coat over a mauve blouse and tweed skirt. A film badge dosimeter, to record radiation levels, was attached to her lapel.

'This is my assistant, Dr Linda Benson,' smiled Kurnitz. 'She is a biochemist, and a Senior Health Physicist, and a very wise young lady.'

Linda Benson pouted at him and smiled at Hugo, offering her hand. 'How do you do, Dr Brill,' she said, 'I know an old colleague of yours, Euan Williams.' Hugo stood up and shook her hand.

'Old Williams!' said Hugo, 'I haven't seen him for twenty years!' He suddenly felt comfortable with them. He was with his peers, back home with academics, none of this touched the nightmare world of Fallon and Rogers. 'How is he?'

'Fine,' smiled Linda, then was serious again. 'We have

117

just over twenty-four hours,' she said to Kurnitz, 'then it's Stage Two.'

'I see,' said Kurnitz, still looking at Hugo. 'Will you fetch me the genealogical chart, Linda?'

She went to a large cupboard and opened both doors. Inside were dozens of large wall charts hung up on a rail, like suits. She expertly selected one, closed the cupboard, and hung the chart on a hook on the door. It was a family tree with multiple branches, running into three generations, all clearly demarcated in different colours.

'You see what can happen in twenty-one years, Dr Brill,' said Kurnitz.

'You mean they were allowed to breed?' said Hugo, looking from one to the other in disbelief. 'In there?'

'Encouraged to breed. Why not?'

'But I thought . . . well, doesn't radiation cause sterility?'

'Yes,' said Kurnitz, 'but not for the Windscale sixteen!' He shrugged. 'But then, neither had they been killed by the lethal dose of 600 rem. It was, as the Americans say, another ball game. We had no choice but to keep them in there while we tried to solve the mystery of their survival. Domestic living units were assembled with all the necessary comforts. Food was no problem, but we decided on an organic, vegetarian diet, free from any kind of synthetic content, because we dared not upset the chemical balance that sustained them. The plant stacks seemed to filter in enough oxygen.' He shook his head. 'We wanted to keep them as they were. A very delicate balance.' He indicated the top of the chart. 'Now! Here was the problem! We had four women and twelve men, living in close proximity.' He winked at Linda.

You old dog, thought Hugo.

'Four of the men had been happily married, Barratt, Roberts, Williams and Jacques, and they remained celibate. Surprisingly enough, we found they were sustained by the love they felt for their wives. But the other eight had appetites which, in this respect, had not diminished. John Garland paired off with Mary Gregory, who, it turned out, had loved him patiently from behind her typewriter for six years. A young fireman named Beakin coupled with a student pharmacist named Penny Wild. Judy Wright, graduate physicist, fell in love with two sturdy firemen, Scott and Westbury, and kept them both happy. And Liz Brown, to our great good fortune, was disposed to enter into a joyous state of polyandry with the remaining four young stallions, and thereby prove herself a credit to the Department of Biochemistry at Birmingham University.'

He chuckled hugely, and winked again at Linda, who gave him a wry smile. She had heard this one many times before.

'And the wonder of it was that they managed to live on these terms, in perfect domestic bliss, for twenty-one years. And still do,' said Kurnitz, determined to enjoy his joke. 'And do you know what, Dr Brill? We write our theses, we climb our mountains, we compose our sonatas, we paint our masterpieces – we reach to the stars and beyond – but I sometimes think that the only true purpose in our lives is to live in harmony with at least one good mate!'

Hugo winced. He had been jolted back to thoughts of Jenny. Oh God, where was she going to fit in with all this? Kurnitz noticed. He put his hand on Hugo's shoulder, rested it there a moment as he continued.

'In the next twenty years, sixty-four children were born to the sixteen founders of the first nuclear colony on earth!'

Hugo ran his fingers through his hair, looking at the chart, not believing.

'This has got to be a very ingenious and rather unholy hoax, Dr Kurnitz. You want me to believe you actually encouraged the birth of sixty-four human beings inside that nuclear cocoon? Let them breed as if they were no more than rabbits under test in a laboratory?'

119

'Something unique had happened in the history of the hominid, my friend. We had no right to interfere, certainly not as scientists. That class of decision we leave to governments – and gods.'

Hugo found he was looking at them more cautiously now, felt less at home. He had just had a basinful of Niven, Pallance and Rains in the remake of *1984*; now, he was featured in *The Island of Doctor Moreau*, with the mad scientist and his Dog-Girl Friday, played by Rod Steiger and Faye Dunaway.

'Bear with us, Dr Brill,' said Kurnitz, his face suddenly wreathing into an irresistible smile, 'it gets worse before it gets better! The sixty-four, first-generation, native-born offspring are not, as you presuppose, human beings! Not in the sense that they are Homo Sapiens Sapiens. Genus "Homo", yes! Species "Sapiens", yes! But Sub-species, "Sapiens Sapiens", hardly.' He held up a photo for Hugo to examine.

'But this,' said Hugo after scrutinizing it for some moments, 'this, surely, is Neanderthal Man! The supra-orbital torus, the bony brow ridge – although that widened bridge to the nose doesn't match the usual reconstructions. Low, sloping forehead, heavy jaw, receding chin. Probable brain size, 1450 cc, which is 50 cc up on us! A classic Neanderthaler!'

'Top marks, Dr Brill,' beamed Kurnitz. 'And we have sixty-four of the ugly devils, under control conditions, all to ourselves!'

'Abba!' Linda was looking hard at Kurnitz, and she was not amused. 'Please!'

Hugo looked from one to the other and was even less amused. 'God in heaven!' he said. 'You want me to believe there are sixty-four prehistoric brutes running around loose inside that bloody cocoon, with sixteen middle-aged Homo Sapiens wondering how the hell to bring up their children?'

120

Kurnitz slapped his knee. 'I like it,' he chuckled, 'yes, I like it! And I cannot wait for your comment on this. A second generation, native born, is under way.' He paused and beamed like a malicious schoolboy unfolding a grisly tale. 'Eight delightful grandchildren, ranging from two to five years old. Here!'

He showed Hugo another photograph. Hugo just sat and looked at it. Fallon's words echoed in his ears: 'You'll have a better idea of the crazy world you've just walked into!' He slumped back in the chair, tilting the photo on his knee, studying it from a distance. It showed a baby of about four months, lying on a bed of ferns. A baby that was normal in every respect, except that a massively disproportionate head, with all the brutish features of the Neanderthal, was sitting on the chunky shoulders like a grotesque, comic mask. It had all the cuteness and charm of a baby rhinoceros, which is not inconsiderable, thought Hugo, but, for the life of him, he could not see any human mother dandling this gargoyle on her knee, waving rattles at it, and making hootchy-kootchy noises. More likely, she would be fixing a muzzle to stop it chewing through her wrist-bone.

'Tell me, if you will, Dr Kurnitz,' he said, 'what was the reaction of the human mother to the very first mutant birth?'

'Ah,' said Kurnitz, nodding approval, 'we didn't of course let her see it straight away. In fact, the gynaecologist who delivered it wanted to wrap it in newspaper, alive or not, and after decontamination, take it straight to the pathology lab for dissection. I was adamant! It must be preserved and reared as a normal child. Fortunately, the first mother was Mary Gregory, a young woman of considerable intelligence and compassion. Within a few weeks she had recovered from the shock and was nursing her child with exemplary love and affection.'

Now we're into *Rosemary's Baby*, thought Hugo, Mia

121

Farrow learning to cherish the unspeakable because Mother Love triumphs over all.

'God in heaven,' he murmured, 'I hope you know what you are doing.'

'No, Dr Brill,' Kurnitz was suddenly serious. 'I can only work on a basis of probability. I have to admit, I do not know.'

Linda Benson spoke for the first time. 'But sometimes our intuition can guide us in place of knowledge or reason,' she said. 'Then we know that what we are doing is right, on moral as well as scientific grounds.' There was a look in her eyes close to spiritual exaltation, Hugo had seen that look before in his early fieldwork in Malaya, the ecstasy of the Shaman, possessed by his familiar spirits. He had seen it in cultist meetings in Los Angeles, the disciples of Synanon and Scientology. He had seen it in London, with Moral Rearmament and the Salvation Army. He had seen it wherever the latest Messiah had popped up in one of his multifarious, modern forms, presumably to save lost souls, more tangibly to open Swiss bank accounts. That look, cold and shining as steel, had always made Hugo feel uncomfortable. It was no different now. Linda Benson may have started out as a dispassionate scientist – now, she was also an evangelist. But even if he felt the same way, Kurnitz would admit to none of it.

'Linda,' he said, polishing his glasses, 'let us keep to the point! The scientific point! Let Dr Brill make his own value judgments. At this moment, I am more concerned to sum up the effects and possible causes of a scientific miracle.' He replaced his spectacles and placed his finger-tips carefully together. 'In a word, Dr Brill, how did the original sixteen survive that lethal dose of radiation, and then manage to persist and procreate for the next twenty-one years? I straightaway discount the idea that it was merely a fortuitous accident, a freak, a one-off change that defies all scientific

122

inquiry and explanation.

He spoke now very slowly, with great care and deliberation.

'No, my theory is this: that that particular quantity of radiation created inside No. 1 in 1957, that specific amount, 612 rem of transferred energy, affected the biochemical behaviour of their cells at a critical level that produced a spontaneous mutation of the species, Homo Sapiens Sapiens, which survives in a low radioactive environment, into a new sub species capable of surviving in a highly radioactive environment, say Homo Sapiens Irradiatus! I repeat, I say quantity, not quality of radiation! This because – and this is already common knowledge – the life forms on this earth have always existed in a radioactive environment. In our present atmosphere, there is a continuous background level of ionising radiation of 100 millirem a year. It is made up, in part, of the formidable energy from the cosmic rays that shower down on us from outer space, penetrating sometimes hundreds of feet below the earth's surface. When you add to this the rays of the sun, though ultra-violet is cut off by the atmosphere, radioactive uranium-238 and thorium-232, which are widely spread in the earth's crust, carbon-14, radium-226 and potassium-40 which we ingest in our food and water, it is hardly an exaggeration to say that there is nothing on this earth that is not, to some degree, radioactive. And that includes man himself!

'The question is, have we merely learned to live with it, or do we in fact *need* to live with it? Darwin postulated that Natural Selection is determined by the survival of the fittest. But fittest for what? Floods? Ice? Drought? Conflict between species? There has always been something conveniently vague about the proven cause of the extinction of a species. But suppose – just suppose – that *the level of radiation was the causal factor*! Suppose the dinosaurs

123

lived at a high level of radiation for the one or two hundred million years that they survived, until it dropped below the level at which they could exist. As happened to John Garland when we brought him out of the reactor building twenty-one years ago. In other words, we are not looking at a theory of Natural Selection, but a theory of *Radioactive Selection!*'

'My God!' said Hugo, forgetting the effect in discussing the cause, 'now that, Dr Kurnitz, is all too blindingly possible! All the major generic mutations of pre-history brought about by significant variations in the level of radiation, decreasing steadily from the atomic whirlpool that existed when the earth broke away from the sun!'

'You have it!' said Kurnitz, beaming with pleasure. 'But there is more. It is not purely an environmental cause! The species itself must be biochemically ready! That is, first there must be a gradual increase, or decrease, in the irradiation of the tissues, to prepare the species for the adaptive leap! Consider it. Since the war, we have recklessly increased our normal background level of, say, 100 millirem a year, to Maximum Permissible Doses up to 75,000 millirem! We have achieved this master stroke by the use of man-made radio-isotopes, nuclear reactors, X-rays, and, by no means least, nuclear weapons, which have generously bequeathed their fall-out of strontium-90, caesium-137, iodine-131 and carbon-14, into the cosy confinement of the human cell. So it is hardly too much to suggest that the Windscale accident precipitated a mutation in an already prepared species. That is, a species virtually inoculated with radiation, and, unlike homoeopathic medicine, encouraging rather than preventing the disease.'

Disease, thought Hugo, a rash of monsters, a tumour of brutes, bottled up by this madman in a nuclear test tube.

'If you are right,' he said to Kurnitz, 'we are all heading for the big change in the next global war.' He shook his head, unable to resist the feeling of nausea. 'If the level of radiation is right, the freak will inherit the earth.'

Kurnitz winced at the pun, did not laugh. 'Not freaks, please, Dr Brill! The citizens of our nuclear colony are far from that! I take pride in them and I protect them. Particularly since, in the event of a global war, it is highly probable that they alone will survive, and they alone – *alone*, Dr Brill – will inherit the earth.' He paused for a moment, letting this sink in. 'We have conducted experiments, first with monkeys, then with other animals. The results, briefly, were as follows. If a monkey is placed inside the zone for less than forty-eight hours, then brought out and decontaminated, it can survive outside as before, with no ill effects of any kind. We call this Stage One. After forty-eight hours, however, it reacts as Garland did, because in that time it has become one of them, and can only exist inside. It has passed into Stage Two. I cannot explain this, I can only observe the fact. That is, there is forty-eight hours' grace before the spontaneous mutation takes effect. And if we had got the sixteen people out within two days of the fire in '57, they would now be living normal lives in their own homes. Fortunately, this did not happen.'

'Fortunately?' exploded Hugo. 'How can you – ?'

'I presume to think it was fortunate! We have conducted experiments with Stage Two monkeys, to see if they can survive at lower radiation levels. They can in fact survive at 300 rem, half the level inside the zone. This means, Dr Brill,' said Kurnitz, jabbing the air for emphasis, 'that a global war, contaminating our atmosphere at anything over 300 rem, would allow our mutant community to survive outside. It would not be enough, however, to produce the same spontaneous mutation for the rest of mankind, who would thereby, unfortunately, perish!'

'Well,' said Hugo, 'I am content to take my chances with the unfortunate majority. If you're looking for specimens, don't book me a room with bath!'

Kurnitz laughed. 'I have enjoyed talking to you, Dr Brill, and I relish your sense of humour, particularly –' he paused and looked, suddenly, very concerned and apologetic. 'Particularly in view of the circumstances. I have not told you everything. But I hope, later, to persuade you differently. However. Linda, will you please take Dr Brill back to Barnes's office. Oh, and show him the periphery of The Garden on the way.'

He shook hands and went back to the window. He was still standing there, immersed in thought, as Linda Benson ushered Hugo from the room.

'I think that Dr Kurnitz is an – er – extraordinary man, Dr Benson.' Linda did not reply as she led Hugo through a door into the open air. He could see the main gate and security lodge about a hundred yards to his left. His Peugeot was parked in the turning area. My God, they do not miss a trick! He looked at his watch. Three-fifty p.m. He had been here for nearly two hours. It seemed like two million years!

Still silent, Linda began walking straight forward towards a construction site well over a hundred yards ahead. Hugo found himself unable to speak to her. He was in no mood to be snubbed, and this blonde zealot was capable of anything. At the edge of the site she stopped, turned, and pointed back.

'The Garden stretches from here to the buildings behind the Windscale No. One, and across the compound as far as the main gate. Oh, and "The Garden" is our name for the extended zone.'

Hugo saw that the area she had indicated was quite considerable. But an underground zone of such a size would be impossible to build in total secrecy. Linda anticipated his question.

'The underground construction was carried out under

126

cover of this research and site services project. The technicians and scientists involved in our work have sworn a
vow of silence which not one of them has any desire to
break.'

For fear of excommunication, Hugo wanted to say, but
crazy Kurnitz was no longer there to encourage him. Instead, he asked her why the underground zone was called
'The Garden.'

Linda began walking back towards the admin. block.

'There has, I suppose, been a slightly mystical air about
the whole project from the very beginning,' she said. 'And
most physical scientists, contrary to public opinion, are
not averse to biblical allusions.' She walked in silence for a
moment. 'It began when the biologists began their tests
with animals, first with the monkeys, later with cats and
dogs, which also served as pets. All breeding strictly controlled, for obvious reasons. Then one day someone pointed
out that the animals were going in two by two, and
christened it "The Ark".'

'Waiting for the nuclear flood,' observed Hugo.

Linda looked at him and inclined her head. 'Very
probably, Dr Brill,' she said. 'Anyway, when the extended
zone was built to cope with the increasing community, the
horticulturalists came into the picture, not to mention the
ornithologists, to experiment with plant life and bird
species. Tropical and sub-tropical plants and birds flourished
in the nuclear environment. It was as if nature had stepped
back seventy-thousand years or more, back to the legendary
"Golden Age". So of course, the humorists were soon
calling it the "Garden of Eden". I think that, very shortly,
you will understand why.'

Hugo dared not let himself think why he would be
expected to change his mind about the things that were
happening under the ground. His heart sank as he remembered the quest that had brought him here. Where

127

did Jenny fit in with this nightmare? Where was she?

They arrived at the front of the Administration block. Linda took him through to Barnes's office. Barnes was sitting at his desk, a grim expression on his face. Fallon and Rogers were standing to one side, looking very much like two schoolboys who had just had six of the best from the headmaster.

'Come in, please, Dr Brill, Dr Benson.' Barnes indicated two chairs. Hugo and Linda sat down. Rogers leaned back against the wall and folded his arms.

'Well, Dr Brill,' said Fallon, 'now you know.'

There was something in Fallon's manner that made Hugo want to punch him on the nose. It was the natural arrogance of the man, now compounded with an air of resentment and more than a dash of bitterness.

'No, Major Fallon,' said Hugo, returning some of the bitterness, 'I don't know! I don't know why you have all decided to let me in on your unwholesome secret! I don't know what I am supposed to do about it! And I don't know, and I dread to find out, what all this has got to do with my wife!'

There was an uneasy silence and nobody moved. Far away in the distance the seagulls shrieked alarms to each other. A solitary car horn sounded.

'Well, where *is* she, damn you?'

There is no silence that is quite like another. For silence is not merely the absence of sound. It is a living thing, taking on its vital quality from the context of life around it. There are restful silences after noise, empty silences framed in boredom, exciting silences overheard at keyholes, electric silences between lovers. But no silence has more intensity and meaning, more tension and dread, than the silence that follows a question that follows a mystery. In such a silence, Hugo waited for his answer.

'Inside The Garden,' said Fallon. 'We let her in.'

Chapter Twelve

Hugo should have known that he didn't stand a chance. He should have known that men like Rogers who lean against walls with their arms folded, saying nothing and doing nothing – nothing but seeing and hearing and watching and waiting – have spent all their lives training themselves to move like coiled springs at the merest nod of a spymaster's head.

Hugo launched himself at Fallon with a strange animal cry that seemed to come from a long way off; it had never before been contained in the resonant cavities of Dr Hugo Brill, placid academic and implacable opponent of violent action. But then Dr Hugo Brill's hands had never before been shaped into hungry claws, reaching to tear out the windpipe of another human being. Dr Hugo Brill's heart had never been filled with unqualified murderous intent, his treasured reason never yielded so willingly to the power and passion of the human nature within.

It was, however, Dr Hugo Brill who felt the blinding stab of pain in his solar plexus, shafts of agony piercing like poisoned darts every corner of his nervous system, dropping him to his knees, crouching him in foetal position like the new-born animal he had become. His arms were steel pincers, forcing against his stomach wall to relieve the pain, as Rogers lifted him up and helped him back into the chair.

'I'm sorry, sir,' said Rogers politely, 'very sorry.'

Cool hands were on his brow. Linda Benson was leaning over him, consoling, gentle. He was feeling sick, trying to retch, unable to find the means in his empty stomach. Yet somehow the humiliation of his physical defeat, the degradation of his intention to kill Fallon, made him feel better. He had sunk to the level of the whole monstrous affair, joined Jenny in the pain and the danger and the indignity of this uncivilised, secret world that they had stumbled into. It had all been beneath him until now, all, somehow, vulgar, disgusting, base, negative, unthinking. Now he was a member of the club, had passed the initiation rites, earned his place in sordid reality, the subtext to the sophisticated dialogues of his Ivory Tower.

Barnes thumped his fist angrily on the table. 'There was no need for this to have happened! No reason for any of this to have happened!' He thumped his fist again, harder, and Hugo looked up, his eyes clearing through tears of pain, to see Barnes staring down Fallon with a look of contemptuous anger. 'You have enough to answer for, Major Fallon, without inciting violence! Damn it all, you dared to ignore Dr Kurnitz's inviolable rule – no human being is ever to be allowed in The Garden without protection! And now this! One more irresponsible act and I shall insist on your immediate suspension.'

Fallon was staring at the ceiling again, his eyes filled with suffrance, only his fists clenching white, to declare the scars on his professional vanity. Yes, thought Hugo, you're not in the field now, you bastard, they've taken away your licence to kill and the habit dies hard!

'Mr Barnes.' Fallon was not giving an inch. 'As I have already carefully explained, there was at that moment no practical alternative. Or should I say, *none less drastic*. Mrs Brill was applying herself to the destruction of the nuclear power programme with all the ruthless skills of a KGB agent or a Marxist traitor.'

'Damn you, Fallon,' Hugo was aching with every syllable, 'Jenny is no traitor, she has never been a Marxist. Damn you!'

'It doesn't matter what she bloody well calls herself, sir, she is doing their work for them! We've had an automatic surveillance on the staff of *Change!* from the first day of publication. Your wife had a dossier a mile long before she even came up here. And the editor, Jeremy Wright, is on a much shorter list and a much shorter leash.' He paused significantly. 'But we can handle that! We just couldn't handle your wife. She was getting too close, dangerously close to "Operation Garden", tying up records of deaths in '57 with the Windscale Fire, probing too hard and too deep in very sensitive areas.' He turned to Barnes angrily. 'A couple more meetings with Jessie Barratt, and she'd have had the whole story.' He punched his arms outwards in exasperation. 'You've had my vote against letting Mrs Barratt inside with her husband; everyone in Gosforth knows her, the cover-up could be risky. But, damn it, now it's a bigger risk to leave her outside!'

Barnes shook his head sharply and said nothing. But Linda Benson spoke. Hugo turned to look, saw the light again in her eyes, the evangelical zeal.

'This one is an exception, Mr Barnes. She should be inside. And after what has happened, I think Dr Kurnitz will be prepared to revise his policy.'

'You are wasting your time, Dr Benson,' snapped Fallon. 'The barons of Whitehall tie our hands with their purse

131

strings, then demand results that they deny us the muscle to bring in! You said it yourself only last night, Dr Brill.' Fallon turned to Hugo with the barest trace of the old twinkle in his eye. 'A deterioration in the quality of war, no formal declarations, no meeting of armies, no battlefields to be hallowed, but the back-street war is on. If they want it contained by a peace-time policing operation, why in damnation bring us into it!' He paced up and down a moment, then breathed deeply. 'Let me give you some idea, Dr Brill, of the full insanity of this situation, the miracle by which "Operation Garden" has been kept secret for twenty-one years. When the fire happened in '57, it was kept out of the press. "D" notices don't seem to incense the defenders of civil liberty quite as much as surveillance and search. But sixteen people were inside the reactor building, sixteen people with relatives and friends who had to be told that their loved ones had died in the fire, that their deaths were top security and must stay that way.

'Tony Frewin had that job,' he nodded to Rogers, who raised his eyes to heaven. 'And he was given plenty of time, soon afterwards, to recollect it in the tranquillity of his retirement. A fortune was paid out in clandestine compensation, "moves" were made from the district, "funerals" with empty caskets laid on at respectable intervals in the next couple of years. But the one date people don't like to lie about is the date on a tombstone. And your dear wife, Dr Brill, was already on to two of those. The one really weak link, however, the Achilles heel, was Jessie Barratt. She suffered from angina, had already had one heart attack, and the news of her husband's death would certainly have killed her. So Frewin decided to tell her the truth. They allowed her to see Barratt through the viewing port, talk to him on her word of honour that she would never tell. So began the weekly visits which have kept Mrs Barratt inconveniently alive for the last twenty-one years. She has kept her word so far, but then, it has never been put to the test!'

'Mrs Barratt will never tell, Major Fallon.' It was Linda again, the true believer. 'She finds The Garden a greater source of spiritual strength than any place on God's earth. She believes The Garden is the Second Coming, and its protection a sacred trust. She will never be less than worthy of it.'

Hugo stared at her in horror and disbelief, looked to the others for condemnation of this bizarre ecstasy. Eighty-eight freaks and mutants, marinating in 600 rem, a Second Coming? And Jenny in there with them? And nobody giving a damn? What the *hell*!

'Now just one moment,' he roared. 'I think I am going out of my mind! My wife is inside that bloody incubator and God knows what they are doing to her in there! And all you talk about is security and the Second Coming! For heaven's sake, will somebody tell me how she is?'

They were all staring at him, expressionless. Only Fallon nodded agreement, almost seemed relieved that somebody else was in touch with reality.

'Don't worry, Dr Brill, they haven't eaten her. Not yet. And I still say it was her own damned fault. She was on to Jessie Barratt. And she would have eventually got through, oh, yes, Dr Benson, she would have found the way. And if you remember, we all decided, *all* of us, to take a gamble and warn her off. We interviewed her quite reasonably, I think.' Rogers nodded. 'And only then did we all agree – *all* of us –' he looked at Barnes again, meaningly. 'All of us agreed that nothing we could say or do would persuade Mrs Brill to give up.'

'So you decided to murder her,' muttered Hugo. 'Or isn't that a term that you like to use in the trade?'

'I prefer to say we decided to teach her a lesson.'

'*You* decided that, Fallon!' snapped Barnes, 'and it was not in your power to do so! Now we find ourselves in this

133

damnable mess and have been forced to implicate Dr Brill into the bargain!'

'I'm surprised you didn't let me in too,' said Hugo, then caught the look in Fallon's eye. That alternative was hardly ruled out even now.

Barnes shook his head and breathed deeply. 'The only danger we face from you, Dr Brill, is that you are deeply in love with your wife. You were a threat to us and you forced our hand, just as she did. Quite incredible to see two minds so tuned in together, leading you both to the same conclusions. Except that you are a man of reason, with no axe to grind, no left or right wing affiliations, and no unmanageable urge to put the world to rights.'

'How can you be sure of that?' Hugo was challenging them not to stand him up and count him with Jenny.

'We had to take the risk. But now we're pretty certain; ninety percent. Enough to be assured of your cooperation once you knew the full story.'

Hugo was shaking his head, staring at the floor. 'I still don't believe it. It must be one of the most grotesque stories that I have ever heard. But I have to admit, I see no purpose in exposing it. It would benefit nobody, and certainly not those pitiful creatures inside. In fact, there would probably be a public outcry to have them put down.' He looked up at Fallon. 'Why didn't you try *telling* Jenny, blast you! Have a little respect for her intelligence and good sense?'

'We have been discussing nothing else but that for the past twenty-four hours.' Barnes shrugged and looked at Linda. 'Anyway, there she is inside The Garden. And we need your help.'

Hugo looked round sharply at Barnes, but Linda spoke first.

'You see, Dr Brill, your wife has been inside for less than twenty-four hours. She is still in Stage One. Stage One monkeys return to our level of radioactivity with no ill effects. There is no scientific reason to believe that your wife would respond differently.'

Hugo forced his right hand away from his stomach, flexing the fingers to restore circulation. He winced, his whole body ached still from the blow. So that was it! Stage One monkeys. Stage One humans. They needed a guinea pig. A human guinea pig! Only Barnes had protested, nobody else! And Fallon had said, '*We* let her in.' So how much collusion was there here between Fallon and Linda, the spy and the fanatic? Kurnitz, even? Was this why the weirdos had let her in, to frighten her into silence, *and* to test their sick theories on the first human guinea pig? Two birds with one hideous stone? It wasn't the time to say what he thought, he'd play the bastards at their own game.

'What do you mean, you need my help?' he said softly.

'First of all,' said Fallon, 'we assume we have your solemn promise that when you leave here you will mention nothing of this to anyone, nor make any written or other record of your experiences.'

'Go on,' nodded Hugo.

'We then want you to go into The Garden, in fully protective suiting of course, and persuade your wife to swear, on whatever oath she recognises, that she will do the same. That is, if we are to release her, hopefully intact. Furthermore, we want her to get her hooks out of nuclear power once and for all and leave us alone!'

Hugo pulled his left arm free, flexed the fingers, examined his bloodless hand for a few seconds, then looked up, smiling.

'Since you have obviously put that proposition to her in the last twenty-four hours and been resolutely rejected, what makes you think I'd do any better?'

'Because,' said Fallon, 'there is now a considerable difference. We have involved *you*. If you can't persuade your

135

wife to give her word, she stays inside. But if she stays inside you are no longer a reliable security risk. You're going to go out alone and stir up heaven and earth to have her out, aren't you, old man? So we will have the problem of deciding what to do with you. And that may be of sufficient concern to your wife to make her change her mind.'

Hugo looked across at Barnes, the Crown Servant, responsible to the Ministry, the people's Tribune, the Guardian of democratic procedure, looked across for his support, found only eyes averted, staring down at the table. The knife edge, thought Hugo. The point, outside the rule of law, at which expediency tips us into the totalitarian state. Barnes needs this as much as Fallon, their jobs are all on the line. That's why Fallon has been kept on. For all his protests, Barnes is in it with the rest.

Hugo leaned back, and pressed his hands on the arms of the chair, forcing himself up. He groaned and sank back, tried again. As he stood, he arched his back and the pain began to subside.

'Good thinking, Major. Love conquers all. The hostage is willing. But will Jenny Brill, Girl Ecologist, give up all for love? Let's go in!'

Linda Benson was at the 'phone, lifting the receiver, asking for Room 11. He could hear Kurnitz at the other end.

'He'll go in,' she said quickly.

'Excellent,' came the metallic answer, 'I'll see you in Control "B".'

The delegation of civil servant and scientist and spies and hostage moved swiftly; down in the lift, along the corridor, through the iron grill into the radio-chemical centre at the foot of Windscale One. For all his inner anger and dread, Hugo found himself curiously excited, almost eager in his anticipation of the adventure. He was Sydney Carton, going to the guillotine, the words of the peroration running

136

around his head like a cracked record: 'It is a far, far better thing that I do, than I have ever done.' He turned them over as the group went into the control base, up a spiral staircase into Control Room 'B', found himself saying them, unexpectedly aloud, as Kurnitz came across to shake him fervently by the hand.

'Well, Dr Kurnitz, it is a far, far better thing that I do, than I have ever done.'

Kurnitz chuckled gleefully and finished it for him.

'It is a far, far better rest that I go to, then I have ever known.'

'I hope not,' frowned Hugo, expecting another facile laugh. But Kurnitz merely nodded at him with a whimsical shrug and a lift of his eyebrows, and hurried him across to the monitoring section. Linda was waiting for them. Barnes and the two security men were hurrying off along another corridor.

'They are going to the viewing ports alongside The Garden,' she explained, 'and Dr Kurnitz and I will come with you. We shall be wearing these plastic suits, and breathing masks with independent air supplies, so you can move around freely. The suits are fitted with two-way radio contact, linking the three of us and the control room. When we reach your wife, we shall leave you to speak to her. You can then turn this switch to the personal PA system, cutting us off and communicating only with her.'

'Thanks for the privacy.' Hugo checked his controls, wondering how Fallon could have been persuaded to relinquish even one word of his conversation with Jenny.

The plastic suit fitted easily, ballooned out generously over his clothing. He found himself staring wide-eyed as Linda helped him on with the overshoes, tying them firmly in place. Tractable and acquiescent, like a dependent child, he stood silent as she fitted him with the breathing mask, turned on the oxygen cylinder on his back. He found he could move easily, see clearly through the clear plastic face of the mask, guessed at his appearance only from the sight of Linda and Kurnitz, transformed, all at once, into bulging, silver Michelin men at his side.

His heart was thumping as they entered the air-lock, stimulated by a mixture of fear and wonder and the avid desire to see Jenny again. It is a far, far better thing – oh, God, Jenny, where are you? He closed his eyes in prayer, no words, only the fervent wish in his heart to see her face, let her know he had found her.

The exit door in front of them glided open and the two scientists moved out into the half-light beyond. Hugo hesitated, only a moment, and followed.

It reminded him, as it had reminded Jenny, of Leptis Magna, the Roman ghost city on the north coast of Africa. He remembered how they had once wandered together through the majesty of those ancient ruins, hand in hand, not saying a word. No need, each had known what the other was thinking. Now he was wandering through this nightmare ruin, looking for her, wondering what he would find, not knowing what to think. He looked up and saw that the light was coming from the large windows of the control rooms above them.

'We are in The Ark, Dr Brill.' Kurnitz's voice came over with unexpected fidelity inside the mask. 'This is where it all started. This is where the animals came in two by two, but we had to work it a little differently for the humans, eh Linda?' Hugo didn't need to look, he could guess the expression on Linda's face, had a sudden, fleeting image of Kurnitz chasing her round a desk. And he was beginning to find the man's sense of humour a little too black and tasteless. It was enough to have bred seventy-two prehistoric throw-backs, without labouring the innuendoes.

'We are now in a radioactive atmosphere of 612 rem, Dr Brill.' Linda's voice was cool and authoritative. 'The

138

protective suiting is triple safe, but we must allow ourselves only thirty minutes before we return to the air-lock.'

Why the hell do we need all these precautions, when Jenny is out there unprotected, Hugo wanted to say. If Stage One is good enough for her, it's good enough for us.

'You must understand, old man,' said Kurnitz, crossing to him, reading him again with remarkable insight. 'We have no reason to doubt your wife's safety in Stage One. But the long-term effects are still under test. That is one of the reasons why we cannot, intentionally, allow any human being to come in without protection. To date, there is no evidence of any long-term damage to our monkeys. So please don't be concerned. Bring your wife out and I will stake my reputation on her continuing good health.'

Hugo nodded, his mouth tight, thinking his private thoughts. It wouldn't be the first time that a crazy scientist had staked his reputation on a human guinea-pig. First animals, then, by some means, people. He wanted Jenny out so he could run her over with his damned instruments. That chilling phrase, 'long-term effects still under test'! Test, test, and double test, the end of all scientific action, blast him! But in that case, why didn't they just bring her out and keep her in confinement – under observation? Nothing added up!

Hugo followed them mutely through The Ark, circling the dull, red housing of the dead reactor, awed by the shattered brickwork and twisted metal of the discharge face, gaping like a malevolent jaw that had spewed out its radioactive venom at the instant of its own destruction. He began to feel it around him, the silent, insidious, unseen presence of the ionising radiation, the invisible army of alpha particles, beta particles, neutrons and gamma rays, mindlessly attacking the seams and crevices of his plastic suit; blind, microcosmic energy doomed to bring destruction and chaos to everything in its path for thousands and thousands of years, revenging itself on man, who, in his blindness, had uprooted it from the relative stability of its natural state.

'Now, now, Dr Brill,' Kurnitz's voice had dropped to a whisper. 'Remember, it is only a quantitative difference. You have been surrounded by radiation all your life, you are a radioactive organism yourself. Do not be perturbed by the increase in dosage, particularly one that is, by some miracle, supportive of life.'

The man is uncanny, thought Hugo. He always seems to know what I am thinking. But the words relaxed him, the nightmare images faded, his panic subsided. Was Kurnitz a lunatic or a saint? Nothing added up! He allowed the Doctor to use up a few of their precious minutes, showing him the wooden huts built to house the sixteen in the early days, the canteen where they had been found alive and well in 1957.

'And the marvel is,' Kurnitz was chattering, his voice high again with excitement, 'the food they were eating, the air they breathed, was contaminated. Internal as well as external irradiation, with no ill effects!'

They were approaching a large arch, spanning a small gauge railway that led out of The Ark.

'This is the supply system, taking food and materials into The Garden. We load them on to radio-controlled containers, outside, and send them in. This is how Mrs Brill was allowed to find her way in yesterday, alone. Now you must persuade her to come back with us! Come!'

Hugo's heart missed a beat, he was sweating inside the suit as he followed them down a steep incline and into the arch. Must persuade her to come back with them? *Must* persuade her? He knew she was stubborn but not insane. And only a lunatic would accept a living death rather than forgo a principle. Only a lunatic. Or a martyr? Not quite. Martyrdom is a public act and Jenny was making her stand very much in private.

A voice from the control room intoned: 'Five minutes.'

'Plenty of time,' chuckled Kurnitz. 'Come!'

As they passed out of the arch, the ground levelled off and the light was suddenly intensified sharply. Hugo blinked and looked upwards for its source.

'Simulated daylight, my friend. The Garden has a dome-like roof, incorporating a planetarium and an ingenious system of lighting and temperature controls. That is how we accustom our Neanderthals to the dawns and dusks and days and nights – not forgetting the stars and planets – that will be waiting outside when the time comes for them to leave. What you see in here is an exact reflection of the state of the heavens outside. For the same reason we encourage them to wear clothing. Fibrous materials fragment too quickly, so be prepared to see some rather natty silver suits of nylon beta fabric.' He nudged Hugo and winked through his visor. 'A great pity, I was hoping to run The Garden as a nudist colony.'

Hugo had to smile. A mad scientist, playing God, with at least the saving grace of humour.

'Well, Dr Kurnitz,' he said politely, 'your children appear to be well prepared for the Promised Land.'

'They are learning fast, Dr Brill. But Exodus is a little way off. At the moment we are content with Genesis. Welcome to the Garden of Eden!'

Chapter Thirteen

The impressions that crowded in on Hugo within the next few moments of his life were like nothing that his wide-ranging mind had ever before encountered. Nor could he fix them in his experience, pin them down, equate them, find parallels in the primitive societies where his fieldwork in Social Anthropology had taken him. Four years with the Tutsi tribe, rulers of the pastoral Kingdom of Rwanda, east of the Congo, had earned him his Ph.D., and the capacity to live with ease in a culture that was, extrinsically, totally distinct from his own. But this was all new, unique.

The impact of the sub-tropical flora dazzled him – he had expected nothing like it – Jenny would have said it was like walking into a Rousseau painting; Hugo would have added, with overtones of Stanley Spencer. It was stylised, shaped, arranged. Arranged! That's it, Disneyland! Bloody Disneyland, a man-made, synthetic Garden of Eden, and all the inhabitants would be robots, programmed by silicon chips, or tricks of the hologram that weren't even there. He ducked as a macaw swooped down at him in a flurry of blue and orange feathers, then soared up to perch in an acacia tree to his left. In seeing the bird, he became aware of the sounds of birds, trilling and chirping and craking all around him. And for a moment he heard the other sound, the human sound, soaring up like a heavenly choir from a Hollywood film, then fading to nothing. He looked upwards, half expecting to see the Tannoys piping in the background music, but there was none. Only the branches of the trees and the bright colours of the birds. And dozens of exquisite orchids, glistening on the upper branches, lower down, ferns and mosses; all epiphytes, taking no food from the trees on which they live.

'They give beauty and all they ask is light.' It was Kurnitz again, still tracking Hugo's thoughts with the same uncanny skill. 'There are not that many birds and animals here, for obvious reasons of space and hygiene, only those selected as pets by the residents. Every animal is known, every creature has a name. They are brought in, new-born, in pairs, and reared here. They mate, and the offspring are taken out in Stage One for observation by our radio-biologists. Three years ago we introduced the first lion cubs – they are still as tame as kittens. There are no predators here, no poisoners, no crushers, no killers; by choice, there are no pests, no scorpions, no mosquitoes and no snakes of any kind.' Kurnitz suddenly laughed again. 'No, Dr Brill, there are no serpents in this Garden of Eden. They would wreak havoc, and I keep them out!'

A humming-bird whizzed by, a spider-monkey hanging from a branch idly swung a matchstick arm at them as they passed. The first adobe hut came into sight, with its reds and browns and yellows and blacks, its thatched roof and its primitive murals. Hugo found his initial notions of detraction and disdain were fading fast, and taking his fears with them. Man-made, perhaps, but there was no

143

commercial calculation behind all this. No, it was a mind that made nice choices, a mind with good taste. Kurnitz? Was this Kurnitz's baby, his very own Garden of Eden? He turned to look at the scientist, found himself expecting a reply to his thoughts. But Kurnitz was moving ahead, faster now, waving Hugo to follow.

The foliage thinned suddenly, and they were in a wide clearing of lush, green grass, almost certainly in the middle of The Garden, a kind of village square. But the first village square Hugo had ever seen with a baobab tree in the middle! It stood there, towering like a great, fat turnip, torn out and replanted upside down. Its root-like branches were covered with leaves, and succulent, white flowers peeped modestly out from behind them.

'Meet Old Baobab,' chuckled Kurnitz. 'We brought him here twelve years ago from Central Africa, a two-foot sapling. Look at him now!'

Old Baobab is their god, mused Hugo. This is where they carry out their tribal rites and sacrifice social anthropologists.

Around the tree, a group of silver-clad figures clustered looking down at something. One of them turned and saw the three strangers and began to move towards them.

Hugo gazed in wonder at his first sight of Homo Sapiens Neanderthalensis. The thick-set brute came slouching, slowly, its head thrust down and forward, the great brow ridge above the eyes leading, like the horn of a rhinoceros, to make first contact with the enemy. Its neck was thick and inflexible, so that the head was unable to turn upwards or sideways independently of the shoulders. It gave the creature a strange kind of nobility, in spite of the lumbering, slovenly gait, in spite of the incongruously modern one-piece suit of silver material that made it look like a circus clown. For all its brutish features, he felt no sense of danger. And then he realised why. There could be no danger from this creature because its eyes, set, small and piggy, in deep sockets each side of its huge, wide bridge – its eyes were those of an *idiot*!

Oh, my God! The cretin of the Alpine valley, the moron and the mongoloid, Simple Simon and Sad Sack, every man's picture of a blinking idiot, were these to be the inheritors of the earth? Was this thing with its silly eyes and its eager smile, its limp wrists and its fawning posture, was this to be the new Lord of Creation? Hugo looked round to Kurnitz almost in supplication, begging him to deny it. But to his astonishment, Kurnitz was smiling at him with a mixture of affection and compassion, like a father taking his son to the zoo for the first time.

'Would you believe,' he said, 'that these ugly devils are cleverer and nicer by far than we are? For all his brutish looks and crude features, Neanderthal man was a highly intelligent and sensitive being. He developed the first religious ideas and made the first great technological advances. About 40,000 years ago he disappeared and our own sub-species took over. Well, my friend, I suspect that Nature has realised her mistake and decided to give Neanderthal man a second chance. Cain slew Abel, and now, be it mutation or miracle, Abel is reborn!'

'Then heaven help him,' said Hugo, 'because if Cain finds out about this, he will slay Abel all over again!'

'Which is precisely,' said Kurnitz, 'why it must never be known!' He approached the brute and switched on his PA. 'Good afternoon, Matthew,' he said, and bowed.

The creature bowed in return and spoke. Hugo closed his eyes and didn't believe it. It was all a gigantic hoax, this was without question a robot run by remote control, the rich, deep, resonant tones, the excellent baritone, speaking excellent English, had to be a recording.

'Good afternoon, Dr Kurnitz,' said Matthew. 'He is in the Library. May I take you to him?'

145

'Thank you,' said Kurnitz, and nodded to Linda. She tapped Hugo on the shoulder, flicked on his PA switch, and pointed to the group beneath the baobab tree.

'We'll see you in about fifteen minutes, we're going to meet John Garland in the Library. Oh, and good luck.'

Kurnitz waved and went off, his arm on Matthew's shoulder. Linda followed. Hugo was alone.

He was walking over to the group, faces were turning towards him, Neanderthal faces, all with the same silly eyes and slack-mouthed grins, like the inmates of an asylum staring at their visitor; silver bodies were moving away as he approached, fading slowly from his consciousness, leaving him alone with the figure seated on a bench beneath the baobab tree; a figure in faded jeans and a loose denim blouse, short, dark hair, and the beloved face of Jenny.

She looked up at him for a second, peering through the visor of the mask, a second only, looking and peering, and then she was in his arms.

'Oh, *Hugo*! Darling, *darling* Huggy!'

'Jenny, my love! Thank God you're safe!'

He could feel her slim body pressing hard against him through the plastic suit, her arms around him, holding him tight and close, holding him with all her might.

'My love. My love,' he said, and held her in a crushing embrace, held her as long as his lungs would let him. Then, with a deep intake of breath, he moved his head back and looked down at her. She smiled up and kissed the front of his plastic visor, her nose and face flattened against it, like a child against a shop window. He kissed the other side, seemed to feel the warmth of her lips coming through, wondered when this silly game would be over and they could take each other to bed for a hundred years.

'Ten minutes!' The voice from the control room jerked him out of the reverie, shocked him back into the six

146

hundred rem of grim reality around them.

'Jenny,' he said urgently, 'sit down a minute.' They were on the bench side by side, her arms still tight around him, her face still smiling up. 'Look, my love; beloved person whom I adore more than anything on this earth, in twenty minutes I have to be back in that air-lock. Do what they ask, shut up about bloody Windscale, swear to keep their secret, anything! But please, my darling girl, come with me!'

She looked up at him, her mouth still smiling, but her eyes unheeding, distant, screwed up in quest of something.

'How did you find me? I knew you would, but how?'

'Oh, Gawd!' Hugo looked heavenwards in despair. 'I can tell you all that later. Please, come out!'

'Tell me now!'

'Jeez! Well, I drove up yesterday morning to surprise you ...'

'Surprise me?' Her eyes twinkled, the wicked angel was back. 'With whom? Hm? Oh, Huggy, Huggy, didn't you trust me?' He looked away. 'There has never been anyone else, my darling, never, never! Never will be!' She hugged him tighter, laid her head against him; he felt her fingers stroking gently through the plastic, relaxed again. She tugged him, the fierce tug of a spoilt child, looked up at him once more. 'But how did you find me?'

'You left a sliver of soap behind.'

'I *what*?'

'In the Cold Pike Hotel – in your room – I found a sliver of soap in the bath so I guessed you hadn't packed your own bag.'

Jenny stared at him for a long moment, her eyes slowly widening, and suddenly let out a loud whoop of noisy laughter.

'Oh, my clever darling, now that really is bloody clever! I love you, I really do love you!'

'Jenny!' He held her firmly at arm's length. 'Do you

realise where you are, soaking up six hundred rem of radiation? If you're not out in twenty-four hours, maybe less, you will be here for life! All your life! Give in, my love, promise to do what they ask. I want you back!' She was looking at him blankly, saying nothing. 'For God's sake, what's so special about the bloody nukes, think about all the other things that need you outside! Including me!'

She spoke at last – reluctantly – as if in a dream. 'I want to be with you so much my love . . . to be with you so much.' Then a small, helpless shrug. 'But I can't do it.'

'Can't *do* it?' Hugo found himself, all at once, on his feet, ripping fiercely at the clips on his breathing mask, his hands trembling and unsteady. 'Right, my bloody-minded, stubborn darling, then I don't wear this silly damned plastic skin for another second! If you can take a dose of this lethal stuff for a lousy principle, then I can take it with you.'

'No, Hugo, no, you mustn't! You can't *do* that! You don't understand!' Jenny was holding his hands with desperate strength, stopping him from tearing away the plastic mask as if her life depended on it, her eyes wide with anguish, pleading.

'You don't think I am going to leave you *here*?' He was shouting now, without concern for his surroundings. 'You don't think I'll go calmly back to London and leave you to throw everything away because you are too proud, too mulish to give your word to these madmen! My God, I'll go back there and raise every roof from Whitehall to Fleet Street!'

'Hugo, Hugo, please! You must never do that!'

'Because of Fallon? Because of what he'd do? With you buried in here do you think I give a damn what happens to me?'

'But Fallon is right! Nobody outside must ever know about this place!'

148

Hugo relaxed his grip, stared at her in sudden shock. *Nobody must ever know about this place?* Did Jenny say that? Jenny, obsessed with her vocation, hunting down injustice with frightening persistence, now sitting on a story that would explode the nuclear power programme into total extinction and swearing him to silence?

'It's nothing to do with giving my word. The Garden must be protected, it is a sacred trust!'

A sacred trust? She was quoting Linda Benson! Word for word!

Jenny saw the expression of horror in his eyes, let go his hands, turned away, speaking almost to herself. 'Oh, dear God, I don't know if I have the strength to say this.'

Slowly, she held her arms up, opened them sideways to encompass The Garden, turning and smiling at him with a radiance that unaccountably had his stomach churning into knots. Jenny had changed! Only now did he realise it. In his craving to hold her he hadn't really looked. She had changed. There was no more of the sadness that had been turning down the corners of her mouth, or the cynicism that had been filtering out the sparkle in her eyes. No more of the bitterness that had been turning his beloved child of hope into a despairing woman, hardened by the blindness and greed of the very species she was fighting to save. All these were gone!

In their place was this radiance that he had seen somewhere before. It reminded him vaguely of Rome; on the night when she had stood on the Spanish Steps, offering her heart to the Holy City, saying the same words she was saying now. But no, by God, it wasn't that look, the joy and exhilaration of a young girl in love! It was the look of religious ecstasy, the cold steel look of devotion and zeal that had chilled him when he first saw it in the eyes of Linda Benson! It was that look that he was recognising now in Jenny's eyes, as she opened her arms wide to The

149

Garden, and said:

'Oh, Huggy, my love, I don't want to leave here! I want to stay forever!'

Chapter Fourteen

Hugo listened in silence. Jenny was speaking fervently, almost babbling, the words pouring from her in a torrent; telling him how she had been allowed to stray into The Garden yesterday after the inquisition, how she had seen the monster and fainted away. Hugo shuddered. That must have been about the time he was driving up from London – wondering who she was with! Fool, Hugo, insecure bloody fool!

'At first it was a shimmering, silver sea, Huggy – then browns and yellows and pinks were pouring into the top of it, mixing and separating into circles and triangles and faces – a circle of faces all around me, a blinding light at the centre – blinding – I lifted my hand – shield my eyes from the glare – looked again – oh, Jesus, that brute face – I *did* see it. . . .'

Hugo's first thought was LSD. Some other hallucinogen? Or amphetamines? Speed? She was on some kind of high, verbalising impressions abstracted from reality, heightened prose, almost poetic. He found himself scrutinizing her eyes, her face, searching for signs of narcotics, dilated pupils, needle marks. What had the bastards done to her? How had they made her one of them? But there was nothing to be seen.

'How long do you think you were unconscious, Jenny?'

'I don't know, but when I saw those hideous faces, I nearly screamed and fainted away all over again. Then something small and soft was tugging at my hand. I looked down, and there was this hideous infant playing games with my fingers. It had a big, ugly head and a gruesome, wide nose with deep sockets each side, and, good grief, I wanted to pull my hand away and run! But, oh, Huggy, then I saw its little eyes! Full of wonder and concern, like a puppy yearning to be picked up and loved. I reached down and stroked its cheek, poor little goblin. And that's when I realised I was lying on a bed of soft fern underneath this fat old baobab ... and that all around me, this horde of monsters in their crazy silver suits were actually not lifting one finger to harm me! So I took a deep breath – and looked right up into their faces!'

She paused to look up at Hugo, searching his face as if to demonstrate.

'And do you know, my darling, I wasn't frightened any more. It was something in their eyes. They weren't savages! They weren't brutes, or killers or cannibals. Far from it; in fact at first I thought they might be a bunch of idiots. But I looked again, and looked down at the child, and saw what it was in their eyes that made me feel so secure, and at peace. They were the eyes of children! Open and innocent, without guile. I smiled, Huggy, and you wouldn't believe it! Great, wide smiles in return, rows of white teeth shining at me, heads nodding joyfully to each other, huge hands reaching out to take mine, offering comfort, reassurance, friendship. And then I heard that sound again, that heavenly, crooning noise, and I realised it was coming from them.

152

They were singing to me! A sort of hymn of happiness and they were singing it to *me*! Oh, Huggy, it was beautiful!'

Sonic vibrations, inducing a hypnotic trance? Music to soothe a savage breast? Was that it? Christ, Hugo, you're getting paranoid! But how else did they keep these brutes in line? How did they brainwash Jenny? Within twenty-four hours?

Jenny was oblivious to any such notions. She told Hugo how John Garland had stepped up and introduced himself and what a shock it had been to see an ordinary human face in the middle of these gargoyles. Then he had introduced his wife, Mary Gregory, and Jenny couldn't believe it because she had read about them in the report of the '57 fire, and neither of them looked old enough to have been senior staff twenty-one years ago. But at least they were humans, and it was like meeting a compatriot in a foreign land. Until they introduced their eldest son, whose name was Plum and whose face was straight out of a text-book on the primordial ancestors of Man.

'He was the first mutant baby and when he was born he was round and red and they didn't know what he was so they called him Plum! Anyway, imagine my further surprise,' Jenny was chattering on, 'when Plum actually apologised to me, in perfect English, for having frightened me out of my senses! What a family! The father and mother looking like an advert for monkey glands, and the son talking like an ape at Oxford! And, heaven help me, I was staring at Mary Gregory with a great deal of the pity one feels for the mother of a mongol child, and she was telling me, with a greater deal of pride, that she had fourteen more like that running around The Garden!'

'I've already told Kurnitz what I think about it,' said Hugo, 'and the sooner you swallow a great deal of *your* pride and give your word to Fallon, the sooner we can get you out of this benighted incubator!' Jenny said nothing, just looked at him. 'Well, damn it all, girl, you *want* to keep this place secret, where's the problem?'

'Fallon!' Jenny almost spat the name. 'He called me up on John's bleeper to tell me that he was delighted to accept responsibility for letting me trick my clever little self into the secret zone and that I had under forty-eight hours before the contamination was irreversible! Imagine that, Hugo, I was shattered! Until that moment I had no idea that I was even contaminated! Then he said that if I wanted to come out unharmed, I was going to swear on oath that I would keep my mouth shut! And that means shut! On the other hand, if I wished to stay bloody-minded and stupid, I would be stuck in here for the rest of my unnatural life!'

That is interesting, thought Hugo. Although Fallon wants Jenny outside and silent, he uses threat and intimidation to force her hand. He could easily have drugged or brainwashed her into submission, but he didn't. *He* wants her outside, healthy and silent! So who has been working on her mind, converting her into a zealot, a disciple of the Great God Baobab? Obviously Kurnitz and Linda Benson! But how? And why? *And why send me in?* Holy Moses, we may end up finding out that Fallon is the only sane ally we have!

'Anyway, John told me not to worry about the 600 rem of radiation, it was quite safe. They have lived in it for twenty-one years without a day's illness. We had a lunch of organic foods and fresh fruit juices in their little home.' She pointedly proudly to one of the adobe huts, tucked away on the far side of the green. 'You must see it, all mod. cons., all electric, no dust! And they eat no meat, neither flesh, fish nor fowl. It was a delicious meal, and John told me all about the birth of The Ark and the Garden of Eden, nine years later. He explained what had really happened in 1957, the truth about the contamination of the reactor building, all about Stage One and Two and Kurnitz's

154

theory of Radioactive Selection and Homo Irradiatus.'

The Birth of The Ark – The Garden – Contamination – Reactor – Stage One and Two – Radioactive Selection – Homo Irradiatus – Jenny's blithe ecstasy had somehow transformed the words into a confession of faith, the proselyte's glib recital of Articles for the new Religion, the Nuclear Credo, revealed unto the Chosen by the Prophet, Kurnitz. It filled Hugo with despair.

'Jenny, listen to me! I've heard it all from Kurnitz, the theories are brilliant but they terrify me. I can see no moral justification for experimenting with these primitive throwbacks merely because, by some freak of science, they will be able to survive an atomic holocaust.' He breathed heavily. 'Which the rest of us assuredly will not. And it doesn't make it any better that Kurnitz has somehow brainwashed them into some kind of simpering civilisation.'

'Brainwashed, Hugo?' She shook her head, smiling, but not telling. 'Throw-backs? No, my love, these Neanders are *truly* civilised and I am proud to know them.'

'Jenny! Now you're talking like Kurnitz! What the hell have they done to you?' The same knowing smile but no reply. 'You really believe in all this, don't you! You think the Nuclear Age is starting right here and you want to play nurse-maid to the apes! Is that it? Well let me tell you, the whole damned experiment is based on a giant misconception! They have all been bred in a controlled, physical environment, fully protected from danger! And, God help us, if our number is ever up and these moronic freaks venture outside their cosy little cocoon, they may wear their natty silver suits and know the difference between night and day, but without experience and awareness of danger they haven't a dog's chance of adapting to our physical environment.'

Jenny was still smiling.

'Now come off it, Huggy, you're getting to be an old

155

cynic. Why don't you just look around you for a moment? Who do you think designed all this, built the huts, planted the trees, raised the animals? They did it all themselves once ·The Garden was built twelve years ago. Does this look like the work of throw-backs and morons? Four of the Neanders hold degrees in Botany, Biology and Horticulture. I think there are five ornithologists and don't forget, the students from Birmingham are physicists and biochemists.' She winked at him. 'But they *are* a bit short on social anthropologists! Anyway, John Garland told me there are thirty Ph.D.s in the Garden, and seven D.Sc.s. Kurnitz submits their papers to a private board. The Neanders, particularly, have IQs over 180.'

'Who does the washing up?'

'Oh, shut up! When the danger comes, your "freaks" won't panic and run around in circles blaming each other. They will use their very brilliant minds. And the Elders will help them.'

'Elders?'

'That's what they call the original sixteen who survived the fire. They are the Guardians, the leaders here, precisely because they are a knowing link with the old world. They know what to expect out there. And there won't be any "civilised" humans left, so there won't be any wars to fight.'

'I see.' Hugo clicked his tongue in grudging admiration. 'Well, I've got to hand it to the old sod. Bloody brilliant. Putting brains into brutes, training them to adapt. But *why*? And what has it got to do with *you*, Jenny, you don't want to breed mutant babies, you're not one of Kurnitz's specimens! What *is* it, Jenny, why are you putting your faith in a man who is clearly more than slightly mad!'

'Abba Kurnitz is not mad.'

'You've met him?'

'We had a long chat this morning. We talked . . . we talked about the possibility of my staying here . . . and . . .

156

and . . . how I would feel if I had to make a choice . . .'

'Between them and me.'

'I don't know . . . Hugo . . . I don't . . .' She sank back on the bench, her eyes suddenly clouding over, the smile gone. She seemed unable to comprehend. 'Abba is not mad. He is a sane man – a kind man.'

'Well, I don't think he is!' Hugo pulled away from her and stood up. 'In fact, I have this growing conviction that Dr Abba Kurnitz is perhaps the most callous and cold-blooded geneticist since Dr Joseph Mengele! He is breeding a race of Neanderthal mutants and training them to take over the earth and set it back seventy thousand years. By that time, it won't concern us, but at this moment it is experimental science at its worst, irresponsible, capricious and malevolent! And it's this moment that matters to *us*, Jenny, for God's sake come to your senses! He wants you here for some vile purpose! Let me take you out of this accursed place and get you back into the fresh, human air!'

She sat there, unheeding, silent, her eyes hollow, defying him. Unable to contain himself, Hugo gripped her arm, pulled her up from the bench. Her body resisted him. She was on her feet but crouching away from him like a whipped dog.

'Jenny, stop this nonsense! Now come on!'

'No-o-o-o-o-o-o!'

The cry came from her with surprising force, stunning Hugo with its intensity. It pierced the air like a dagger, thrusting into every corner, cutting a swathe of torment through the buzz and murmur and serenity of The Garden. There was an instant of terrifying silence. And then Jenny burst into tears.

'Oh, dear God!' Hugo reached out to comfort her but she pushed at him fiercely and turned her back. She was sobbing desperately, her arms raised above her head, her fists clenched hard in supplication.

157

'Go away! You don't *see*! You mustn't touch my faith! Go away!'

Hugo was helpless, shocked into inaction by the hysteria. He had never seen Jenny like this. What had he done – what had those insidious bastards done to her mind?

Then suddenly he was aware of intense activity all around them. He turned sharply but there was no one to be seen. Only flurries and whispers and scuffles in the bushes. Brute faces peering from the foliage and instantly gone. He tried to suppress a feeling of panic. Could the brutes become violent? Attack and kill?

They rose up into view all at once. A circle of Neanderthal men and women, appearing as if by magic, stepping through the screen of succulent plants and flowers to stand motionless at the edge of the clearing. A circle of half-human faces, staring without expression at the creature in the plastic suit and the sobbing girl.

They began to move in. Slowly, one step at a time, slowly closing in like a ring of monstrous puppets, arms hanging limp at their sides, heads thrust forward from the shoulders, powerful and menacing.

Jesus, where are Kurnitz and Linda? Standing back, waiting for the slaughter, making careful notes? Blast' em! Wait! The control room – on the intercom! That's it, call for help, get Fallon on to it! Hugo was about to look down – about to grab for the buttons on his control panel, press the lot if necessary, raise the alarm – when the sound came.

The sweet, strange harmony, the ethereal, indefinable blend of voices that seemed to flood in and around them from the synthetic heavens above. For once in his academic life, Hugo made no attempt to question or explain, cared only that this was some kind of offering of sympathy and comfort, felt only an inordinate sense of relief.

It was uncanny. The faces of the Neanderthals were no

longer brutish. The great jaws were wreathed in smiles of reassurance, the small eyes were tender with concern. They reached out their great hands towards Jenny as if pleading with her to be happy.

Hugo watched, as if he were outside it all, as Jenny's small fists relaxed and opened up, like flowers opening to the warmth of the sun. She straightened up and stood erect, turning slowly, her eyes bright again, the smile back on her lips.

'Oh, thank you, thank you,' she said and touched their hands and faces and they smiled and hugged each other and their voices blended sweeter and they turned and began to move away, back to the forest, as they had come.

'Do you hear them, Huggy? These beautiful people? They came to cheer us up and now they're leaving us together again. *Now* do you see?'

Hugo didn't know what he was supposed to see. A while ago, that shining light in Jenny's eyes had chilled him. Now he was rather glad it was back. While Jenny was smiling he knew he was safe – because he was pretty sure those Neanders didn't give a damn about him. She moved across to him. He put out his arms and held her. The singing faded, the Neanders were gone.

'Very moving,' he said, 'once they got to the Eisteddfod bit. But when they came out of the woodwork, it didn't help to know that they were biochemists and botanists – their looks were against them.'

'You fool, Huggy!' Jenny laughed. 'But did you *see*?'

'See what?'

'I can't tell you, you have to see it yourself! Oh, come on, didn't their music tell you anything?'

'Their *music*? That was their *music*?'

'Yes.'

'You mean that's all? No instruments or symphonies?' She shook her head. 'So Bach and Stravinsky grafted in vain?'

159

'They think the old music is just noise, hammered out by self-indulgent egotists to manipulate the passive majority. The Neander music is aural recognition of their concern for each other. Don't you see now, Hugo? It joins them together, affirms their unity.'

'Oh come on, my love, you can't dump a heritage of artistic achievement because everyone likes to singalong softly in a mud hut. It's regressive, a shocking waste.'

'Not if you don't need it! Don't you see? For these people, their music and painting, all their art, everything is an expression of social love. When I came to The Garden, I saw it straight away.'

'Saw what, for God's sake?'

'Hugo, you are just being obtuse. I know you and I think you do see, but you won't admit it because of me. But you know that something *new* has happened here, something unique and wonderful. You know Kurnitz isn't mad, he isn't breeding a race of mutants to take over the world. Why devote his life to that?'

'Kurnitz would breed rattlesnakes with soprano voices if it proved one of his bloody theories.'

'Damn you, Huggy, I am going to break my word and make you face it! The miracle of The Garden is that these mutants have evolved in a very special way.' Hugo raised his eyebrows. 'They have evolved, my darling, to love each other!'

Hugo looked at her for a moment, then groaned heavily as if he were having a tutorial with a very difficult student.

'Yes, Hugo, everybody here *loves* everybody. You can see it in their eyes, you can feel it in the air, surely you heard it in their music. Homo Irradiatus, the new Man, has not evolved as a brute or a moron, he has evolved as a creature of great brilliance. But most important, he has evolved without evil!' She was close to him now, looking earnestly into his eyes, pleading. 'Oh, Huggy, I want you so much to

160

understand. Don't you see, they are the kindest most beautiful people, a truly loving species. It's the Garden of Eden before the Fall, it really is the Second Coming. Oh, don't look at me like that, please don't be cynical. I was when I came in, but I'm not ever any more. They have given me back my faith!'

Hugo found he was no longer shocked by the reiteration of the Scriptures, the Articles of Faith. He was just looking at her, trying to come to terms with her persistence, the strength of her conviction, particularly with her insistence that he understand, give her his blessing. He had come in to persuade her to give up her attack on Windscale, had expected arguments about journalistic integrity, even stubborn pride. But never this possession with ideas approaching religious mania. At times she had almost convinced him, he knew that the incident with the Neanders had touched him more deeply than he liked to admit. But his damned computer brain had stored up all the inputs on phoney cults and fake philanthropists. He had met too many 'messiahs' who spoke with affection and acted with calculation. Maybe he had become cynical. But he lived in a world where one contended in vain with the schizoid smile of 'the decent chap who means no harm', vanity blind to itself, the clouded eyes of the thinker of secret things. His own species had destroyed his faith.

'Jenny, my love,' he said, 'maybe I have become cynical, maybe my faith is gone. And the last thing I want to do is to touch yours. But there's something here that doesn't add up. I can't explain, but I can't buy it either. Of course it's a miracle that the Elders survived 600 rem of radiation. But they are human, Jenny, they are still *human*! They came into The Ark with the full quota of psychological hang-ups and ego-oriented social patterns. They are still Homo Sapiens Sapiens with all the tainted traces of that sub-species in them, and those traces have been passed on

161

to the Neanders. So if anything has converted these primitives into truly loving Noble Savages, your kindly Doctor Kurnitz must have done something to help it on; maybe he played some pretty smart tricks in his operating theatre. It's nothing new. The danger is, when the tricks backfire, there is always a reversion to type. And you are giving yourself up to a lost cause.'

'Oh,' said Jenny, 'I am beginning to understand.' Her eyes were on him, but focusing again on a distant point. 'I am beginning to understand. You can't accept a miracle. You're too grown up. Like Wendy, you can't see Peter Pan any more. So when I tell you about the miracle of The Garden, you are exploring the possibilities of brainwashing techniques, anything from narcotics to surgical implants to explain it away. Right? But I've been here for twenty-four hours, darling, and you've been here fifteen minutes. And you haven't met them properly, you haven't spoken to them. Be fair, Hugo, come with me to the Library. Let them speak for themselves.'

'Fifteen minutes gone.' The control room was on again. 'There isn't time, Jenny.'

'Oh, pooh! Kurnitz told me he sometimes spends whole afternoons in The Garden. You don't even need that plastic suit in Stage One.'

'Dammit, Jenny, I thought that too! You've been here unprotected for twenty-four hours, and Kurnitz said that if I bring you out he will stake his reputation on your continuing good health!' He looked at her, puzzled. 'Yet with you he discusses the possibility of your staying. So what is that old fox up to? Right, Jenny, I'm with you! To the Library.'

They walked in silence for a moment before Hugo spoke again.

'Would I be right to assume, my love, that this plastic suit is not so much to protect me, but to warn the inmates –'

'Inhabitants!'

162

'Inhabitants of The Garden?'

'Yes, Huggy. Kurnitz has made it an inflexible rule that no human is to be allowed in without the suiting and then only for a limited time. This way they are identified as aliens and the Neanders are on their guard.'

'Well, once Kurnitz knew you were here, why didn't he just pull you out? *Kurnitz* is in charge, not Fallon. So what *is* that old fox up to?'

'He congratulated me this morning on seeing the really significant thing about The Garden – the loving species. He said it was very rare. Only certain people see it –'

'The Chosen.'

'Hugo! But they must never be *told*. They have to *see* it for themselves. If they don't see it naturally, they are a bad risk. They could pretend to be loving and in no time at all they would be sewing the seeds of dissention in The Garden.'

'So that's what he meant!'

'Who?'

'Kurnitz! He said there can be no serpents in this Garden of Eden. They would wreak havoc and he keeps them out. So good old Homo Sapiens is the serpent.'

'Good old Homo-aggressive-jealous-acquisitive-murderous-Sapiens.'

'Hard cheese for Homo-loyal-industrious-loving-courageous-Sapiens.'

'Well, he can toss the coin but the dark side comes up two out of three – because it's his natural state. But here, dear cynic, love is the natural state. No deception, no masks, no ploys, no games, no gambits. These people are wide open, all up front and painfully vulnerable. A serpent in this Garden would really wreak havoc.'

'Well, I didn't see what you saw so I assume that I am a serpent,' said Hugo.

Jenny didn't want to answer. She lowered her eyes, kept

163

on walking. Hugo laughed out loud.

'I love *you*, Jenny,' he said.

She smiled at once and took his hand. 'Of course you do, my darling. I asked Kurnitz this morning why I was allowed to remain in The Garden with his enchanted children. And he winked at me and said I was probably being punished – for being one of them. Ah, prepare yourself, my love, we've reached the Library!'

Chapter Fifteen

The whole of the space at the end of The Garden had been given up to the Library, a rambling, wood-framed building, fronted with a colonnade that made it oddly reminiscent of a Greek temple. A wide, grassy bank sloped down from the steps in a gentle, undulating gradient to meet the sub-tropical flora at the edge of the forest. All across it, groups of silver figures were reclining on the grass, rippling and shimmering in the light, like trout packed in a stream, the buzz of their conversation mingling with the muted birdsong and the noises of the forest.

As they approached it, catching their first glimpse through the gaps in the trees, Jenny told him how she had been taken there by the Garlands the previous afternoon and stayed for the rest of the day.

'It was like being at a party with all of my very best friends at once. They greeted me as if they'd known me for years and then they all began to sing that sad, joyous song! So I joined in too! You really do, don't you, I kept saying to them, you really do love each other!'

She told him how the Library was the centre of all activities, stocked by the omniscient Kurnitz with the last word on every subject. A hive of bustling activity and discussion, it was their market-place for ideas, an immaculate safety-valve for the ferment of clashing intellects wandering in from the cloisters of The Garden, sharpened for debate. Here, in their Universe of Truth, their love for each other was no less evident. But there was no cloying sentimentality in it, no suffocating possession. It held them together in a wondrous communion, where the posing of questions and the seeking for answers were the sacred rites. The truth was all that mattered, whoever had it. There was no vanity, because there was no prestige, no deference, because there was no power, no corruption, because there was no wealth. And no casuistry, because there was no need. Only Truth and Love, set in Beauty.

Apart from another call from Fallon on the transceiver, with a further string of threats which the joys of The Garden had by now rendered impotent, Jenny's recollection of the world outside had dwindled to a distant point. A point of debate in a heated discussion on Western decadence; was the permissive seed planted in Marxist soil? A point of departure in a reflective dialogue on the civilisation that would take over.

Everyone had been eager to discuss Jenny's dilemma. Should she give in to Fallon and renounce her freedom to speak her mind, or should she cling to her principles and thereby renounce her world? The discussion had been objective and dispassionate, their only concern was her happiness. But apart from vowing that whatever she decided, she would never speak of The Garden to a living soul, Jenny was hardly concerned with the problem any more. In this community of informed minds and open hearts, she had found her ideal. Outside it, nothing existed.

'Except for you, of course, my love,' she said, holding on

tight to his gloved hand, 'now come on and meet the gang!'

Hugo, embarrassed, and beginning to sweat inside his plastic fancy-dress, went reluctantly. As Jenny led him through the chattering throng, she waved gaily to the Elders and Neanders; and Hugo had to admit to himself, the warmth of their affection for Jenny was impressive. Just as she had said, white teeth flashing away, heads nodding joyously, even a five-bar burst of 'She's a jolly good serpent' by The Garden Glee Club. As for me, Hugo Brill, the Stranger in the Plastic Skin, no more than a courteous nod, a look of awareness. Ah well, I'm not one of them, the Saints have been taught to keep up their guard.

She led him to a group at the far side of the lawn, a group that included Kurnitz and Linda. They were stretched out comfortably on the grassy bank, deep in conversation. And not the least bit concerned that they were in their normal clothes, their protective suiting dumped casually on the ground beside them!

'Well, you devious old bastard,' muttered Hugo, moving forward to place himself accusingly in front of them. He had, at least, the small satisfaction of seeing Linda start up and make a slight move towards her gear. But Kurnitz stayed where he was, head resting back on his hands, smiling benignly up at Hugo as if he had been expecting him all the time.

'Unmasked and undone, Dr Brill,' he said. 'But Linda and I are old friends here and we have special privileges.'

'Of course,' said Hugo, 'and I must remain the Bogeyman from the Big Bad World outside.'

'I am prepared to doubt that, my friend,' said Kurnitz. 'Take off that silly outfit and come and join us.'

Linda turned to him sharply, but he waved her to silence. Jenny gave a gasp of delight and dropped to her knees beside the old man, peering eagerly into his face.

'Can he, Dr Kurnitz, can he really? He understands, you know, he really understands!'

'I know, dear child. Well, come on Doctor Brill, share the elixir vitae with your charming wife and make yourself comfortable.'

Hugo hesitated. Elixir vitae? What was he letting himself in for? He knew that in the last few minutes his notions of hypnosis and narcotics and electronic implants had been fading fast. But he was still on the alert, still watchful for other causes. Elixir vitae. If he breathed the air of The Garden would he too be turned into a steel-eyed zealot? A new subject for laboratory test? Test! Wait a minute! Kurnitz was breathing it! So one thing at least was clear. Kurnitz was *not* looking for guinea-pigs to test the long-term effects of Stage One. He could make all those tests on himself – and Linda. Then why, thought Hugo, do I have this feeling that the old man is up to something, never moves without some very definite strategy laid out in that clinical mind?

Jenny flipped herself up from her knees and peered up through the visor at Hugo. She could barely contain her excitement.

'Oh Huggy, it's an enormous privilege to be invited. You *have* to accept! We'll be *together*.' She whirled around and danced a few steps on the grass. 'Come on, Huggy! Come on in, the water's fine!'

Hugo laughed. He'd come all this way to find *Jenny*. He was going to join *her* and damn the consequences! He reached for the ties on the mask and Jenny was there in an instant, helping him to remove it.

It was off! For a few seconds he stood quite still, trying not to let them see that he was holding his breath. Then – here we go, Hugo! – he was breathing in the contaminated air! Mustn't think about it, off with the overshoes, off with the gloves, off with the rest of the paraphernalia, and Jenny

168

was in his arms, hugging him for dear life!

It occurred to him that he was now able to kiss her and he did. Hugo was normally shy of public display, but not now. Not here. Not with the Truly Lovin' Species. No sir!

'Good, well, that's done,' said Kurnitz, beaming with satisfaction. 'Jenny, introduce the Garlands.'

Hugo shook hands with John Garland, silver-haired but his face unlined and incredibly youthful, and his wife Mary, looking a good twenty years younger. How old *were* they? Jenny tugged his arm.

'And this is Plum Garland,' she said, with the merest twinkle of mischief in her eye.

Hugo took the young giant's hand with very mixed feelings. He was tempted to say 'Plum Garland I presume?' but found himself a little too shy, a little in awe of his first Neanderthal handshake. And it had also occurred to him that the massive head and overhanging brow were really quite noble features. And that those small, helpless eyes were actually blazing with intelligence and sensitivity.

'How do you do, Dr Brill.' Ye gods, it *was* an Oxford accent! 'It's a great pleasure to meet you at last.'

'At last?' quipped Hugo. 'Was I expected?'

'We have been discussing you, Dr Brill,' said John Garland, 'and wondering what you have decided.'

Mary Garland leaned across. 'And we'd like you to know that if you persuade Jenny to leave, we're going to be very sad.'

'Shattered,' suggested Jenny.

'Shattered,' said Plum.

Hugo looked at him for a moment, than at the others.

'What I don't understand,' he said carefully, 'is that Jenny and I are members of the sub-species, Homo Serpent Sapiens.' Kurnitz chuckled and mimed applause. 'And I was under the impression that no serpents are *ever* allowed in this Garden.'

169

'Jenny has never been a serpent, Hugo.' John Garland spoke, then looked at Kurnitz, who nodded. 'She is a Natural Elder, a treasured link between our two worlds, like Abba and Linda –'

'And Jessie Barratt.'

'Yes, Linda, like dear old Jessie Barratt, she is one of the chosen few who quite naturally belong here.'

'And what about me?'

'You, Dr Brill. That we do not know. You are a risk –'

'But you never take risks, Dr Kurnitz! And yet you've allowed me in, unmasked. Why me?'

Kurnitz looked at Hugo and narrowed his eyes.

'We must wait and see,' he said. 'Forget the half-hour limit, that has no validity or purpose now, stay here with your wife and experience, at first hand, the ways of The Garden. Then make your decision together. Can I be fairer than that?'

Jesus Christ, thought Hugo, he is offering us both a one-way ticket! His mind flashed suddenly to all the implications! Jenny's disappearance; Hugo's disappearance, searching for her; all the traces they had left; her family; his family; Jeremy Wright – well, Fallon wanted him shut up anyway; Fallon could fix it all – oh, absolute nonsense, why was he even thinking like this? The air! The bloody contaminated air was reaching his brain! He sat down slowly, leaning back against a grassy mound, looking thoughtfully at Kurnitz. Jenny dropped down at once to lie beside him, her slim body moulded against his, her head nestling in his neck. He hugged her, felt relaxed and content. But his brain stayed sharp as a tack!

'Dr Kurnitz,' he said, 'let's get down to the real issue here. The ways of The Garden I have barely observed, but I trust my wife's evaluation of them. I do not, however, share her blind faith in your experiment. In a word, I want to know how you have produced your very precious

170

eighty-eight Saints. And I want to know why you have let in an accredited serpent who is capable, as I discovered earlier, of precipitating a crisis. In two days I should be in Stage Two but how do you know I'll no longer be potentially disruptive? By that time are you positive I'll turn into an Elder? Is that what you want to test?'

Kurnitz laughed, Hugo thought, perhaps a little too much.

'Oh, I do like you, Dr Hugo Brill. If I were in your shoes I should be asking the very same questions. So I shall be honest with you – I have no idea. I should prefer the word containment rather than experiment. And I am not clever enough to have produced our benevolent friends. But Plum has some ideas, maybe he can enlighten you a little.'

'Ah,' said Plum, suddenly standing up and pacing intently, like a true professional ready to perform at the drop of a hat. 'I have made a comparative study of three great divines, Moses, Jesus and Buddha, since they gave mankind its first conception of the rule of love, two thousand or more years ago. It is particularly significant that there have been no new revelations of this order within the last two thousand years. I do not discount Mohammed, in 600 AD, but he essentially restated the Book of Books, the Mishna and the Gospels, cleansed and simplified them in his own passionate terms. Later divines and prophets have also rationalised the primary word of love into secondary religions. The question is –' Plum stabbed his index finger into the palm of his hand for emphasis. 'The question I *ask* is, what was the level of radioactivity up the mountain or in the wilderness, wherever the simple truth was revealed?'

Hugo suppressed a laugh. Plum was deadly serious. So were the others. And Kurnitz was leaning back, his eyes half closed, beaming with pleasure.

171

'Did Moses climb Mount Sinai,' continued Plum, 'and sit on a rock of uranium-238?'

Hugo couldn't restrain himself, he laughed out loud. To his great relief, Plum chuckled with delight. Kurnitz roared.

'Did Jesus wander in a wilderness of thorium-232? Did Buddha sit under his great tree by the side of a river, ingesting radium-226 and potassium-40 when his vision came?'

'Timothy Leary thinks they all did it on LSD,' smiled Hugo.

'Illusion,' Plum shook his head gravely, 'has never been the father of truth. And love, or anything else, that is bred in illusion, has no life beyond it. Love is bred in the bone. It is a cellular construct, a microcosmic miracle. It cannot be worn like a skin.'

Hugo became aware that Jenny had moved her head, was swivelling her eyes up to watch his reactions. Hugo nodded approval; the Neanders, whatever they might be, were certainly *not* idiots!

'Very well, sir,' went on Plum, 'if it is ludicrous to accept uranium rocks and thorium deserts, we must ask ourselves if the world, two thousand years ago, was not at the same critical level of radiation as we have here.'

'I like your uranium rocks and thorium deserts much better,' said Jenny, wriggling into a position where she could look at Plum. 'Otherwise the world two thousand years ago would have been filled with Buddhas and Jesuses and Moseses.'

Hugo laughed with the others but his mind was tracking the implications of this wild idea.

'Then let us not be specific about dates,' Plum went on. 'Let us consider the fabled Golden Age when all men were divine. And,' he said slowly, savouring every word 'is not the link between such a fabled epoch, and the known instances of Revelation – and what happened here in The

172

Garden to the original Elders – is it not possibly a spontaneous mutation caused by 600 rem of radioactivity?'

'Well, Dr Brill,' said Kurnitz, looking at Plum with unconcealed pride, 'what do you think?'

'You mean,' said Hugo, fascinated, his eyes screwed up in concentration, 'that Jesus, Moses, Buddha, all the great Teachers were *mutants*? That they were destined to wander alone in a world of men who were unable to comprehend the purity of their ideas, because those ideas could only take root in 600 rem? What you are proposing, then, is the Radioactive Messiah.'

'Radioactive Messiah,' whispered Plum, his eyes gleaming. 'Now, that is a very interesting term. May I use it?'

'Of course,' said Hugo. 'But may I continue? You then hedge your bets by suggesting that certain ordinary human beings like Jenny, who have not been subjected to spontaneous mutation – you call them Natural Elders – are also ready for your Kingdom of God on earth. So does that make Jesus a mutant or a Natural Elder?'

Plum was staring at Hugo with a blank expression on his face. Kurnitz came to his rescue.

'The implications of that are far-reaching, Dr Brill. But what really matters is this. There are in the world, men who, for whatever reason, have kindness deep-rooted in their cellular essence, men who are doomed to stand alone "on the shore of the wide world", mocked and reviled by the false inheritors of the earth. We are now certain that 600 rem of radioactivity produces such men. We cannot be sure how many of them exist without it.'

'And for whatever reason,' persisted Hugo, 'the hope for the world lies not in Homo Sapiens but in this new species.'

'I think,' said Kurnitz, 'that we are all agreed on that.'

'You may have noticed, Dr Brill,' John Garland broke in, 'that nobody has aged to any extent in The Garden. I

173

am seventy and Mary admits to fifty-three. And Plum is twenty-one, though I sometimes think he is older than I am. But it is a fact that we have no illness here.'

'Probably,' offered Kurnitz, 'because no disease bacterium or virus can survive in 600 rem.'

'So the Golden Age of Love and Longevity was filled with Radioactive Methuselahs as well as Messiahs,' said Hugo. 'And if I stay a good boy for forty-eight hours I stand a good chance of being a very old Saint!'

'Oh Hugo,' whispered Jenny, snuggling closer, 'if only you would.'

Reclining there, in the midst of the thriving, lively community of The Garden, with Jenny close in his embrace, Hugo had a feeling of euphoria and contentment that he had never before known in his whole life. He believed at last in the miracle. Could he stay here like this, with Jenny, for the rest of his life? Bewitched or not, would that be such a bad thing?

Jenny lifted her head and kissed him. The touch of her small, soft mouth, searching for his, completed his bliss. They were lying there, bodies entwined, swaying imperceptibly together, engendering the first tiny flicker of passion. Everything around them faded to a low murmur; Hugo had no awareness of where he was, no consciousness of the instant when it became inevitable that they should make love. Fingertips were searching, picking at buttons, teasing at cloth, pulling at laces, moving silently, tenderly, to leave them nakedly, consummately, bound together. And then it was as if they were floating, soaring, fusing with the air and the earth; as if they were breaking into tiny particles that raced across physical boundaries to leave them no vestige of separate identity; to lift them to a climax of ineffable passion and love; to bring from their throats a strange, sweet sound rising to a peak of ecstasy, merging into a swelling harmony as other voices blended with theirs. . . .

174

Other voices? The music of The Garden? Intruding into their sacred union, their private act of love? And something else? A physical presence!

Hugo opened his eyes and lifted his face from Jenny. To look into the jagged nose-bridge and simpering pig-eyes of Plum Garland. Hugo started up! Jesus Christ, the brute was naked too! The massive frame was moving towards Jenny, the huge, thick hands reaching for her slim waist.

'You foul, stinking bastard!' screamed Hugo, 'you dirty, vile *animal*!' In one heave, he had pulled Jenny away and sent her rolling across the grass, grabbed one of Plum's rippling biceps in both hands and, with a surge of insane strength, yanked him to his feet! 'You hypocrite!' he shouted. 'You bloody, mealy-mouthed fake!' And he punched his fist with all his might into the Neander's mountainous jaw, to send him crashing to the turf.

It didn't cross his mind that Plum could have killed him with one blow of his enormous fist, he could only gaze down in unconcealed contempt at the trembling giant who sprawled back, holding his jaw, looking at Hugo with an expression of utter bewilderment and despair.

And then Hugo was aware of something else. All around him on the sward were naked bodies, Neanders and Elders, staring at him in astonishment, fixed, as tiny cameos, in the pairs and trios and groups in which they had been making love. John Garland and his wife, as naked as the rest, were at least lying together. But Hugo was not concerned with them.

His eyes stabbed into the melange of flesh and staring faces, looking for the Devil and his Handmaiden. Where were Kurnitz and Linda?

'Where are you, Kurnitz?' It was his own voice but Hugo didn't recognise it. 'Where are you, you rancid old goat? Humping Dr Benson in the bushes? Love? This is your truly loving species? I've got a better name for your dirty-minded mob! Why don't you call them Homo Erectus?'

Oh, Hugo, sick at heart and still making jokes? He turned to Jenny and saw, with some relief, that she was staring round, as shocked as he had been. Thank God it hadn't happened before he arrived.

'Jenny!' He whipped out the order. 'Dress!'

He was pulling on his clothes so fast that he barely listened to Garland speaking at his side, Garland, standing up with no concern for his nakedness, to appeal to Hugo in the same, sweet, reasonable terms.

'You must understand,' he said. 'The Neanders grow up entirely without self-consciousness. Sex is the most natural and beautiful thing for them.'

'In a pig's eye!' snapped Hugo. 'I don't want any more of your sanctimonious shit! Jenny, hurry up!'

She obeyed mutely, gazing wide-eyed at the sprawling bodies, the shocked faces, poor Plum still lying there holding his jaw.

'It's not easy to comprehend, Dr Brill. For you, and us, monogamy is still the only way. But for the Neanders there is no romantic concept of the single, perfect mate, because they are all perfect mates. They were brought up, on Kurnitz's advice, with no marital preconceptions whatsoever – they have all, virtually, married each other. They live with whom they want, when they want, and all the children belong to all of them. But believe us, Dr Brill, it is a blessed union.'

'Don't patronise me, Garland, I've documented enough legitimate cases of group marriage to recognise that this romp is just a shabby licence for free love; at a quick glance it's a full-blown, bloody orgy; and don't tell me it's not homosexual and incestuous and God knows what else!'

'The Neanders are entirely heterosexual, Dr Brill, they see no purpose at all in deviation. Nor is there any incest.

176

They keep their sex in perspective, it is purely an extension of their love for each other. Your act of love touched them deeply and they responded.'

Hugo was dragging on his protective suit. The air in this over-sized bell-jar was laced with some kind of aphrodisiac that must have turned him on. No more molecular Mickey Finns, he had to get his mask back on and get Jenny and himself out fast.

'Admirable,' he growled, 'a new page of history was opened here twenty-one years ago. So you took your chance, started from scratch, no preconceptions, no false values, no heritage of blindness and duplicity – and no respect for another man's wife!'

'Plum was showing his love and respect for you *both*.'

'Oh, you bloody liar. He just wanted to get in on the act!'

'You only had to make it clear that you preferred to be alone.'

'I think I did! Oh, my God, I don't believe all this.' He put his mask on, began fixing the straps. 'Come on, Jenny, let's make a dignified exit from the Garden of Allah.'

'No, Hugo.'

Jenny was looking at him as she had on the Green, he was once more the Stranger in the Plastic Suit, the alien from outside.

'No, Hugo. I'd hoped you would understand, but you don't. I belong here but you don't. I admit all this shocked me at first but John has explained – it's the extension of their love, there is no lust to dirty it. My faith is intact, Hugo. But you still can't see and never will.'

'Jenny, you are a bloody fool! I know I don't belong here. I'm aggressive, I'm a fighter. I want to go back to my rotten world outside and do some small thing to put it right! In here it's all a fake. They dodge the issue, they wrap up their dirty ways in sugared words and *you* can't see. But you will once you're outside. I'm taking you with me. Come on.'

'The noble fighter,' said Jenny, taking a step back from his outstretched hand. 'Is that really it?'

Hugo glowered at her, tried to slow his breathing, pull back to reason, but he knew what was in him, gnawing away at his cherished self-control. She didn't want to come with him and the pain in his love was becoming too much for him to bear.

'No, damn you, it's not! If you stay here for the rest of your life, then sooner or later one of these ugly bastards will offer you his benevolent nature while they're all extending their love, and you, you damned idiot, won't throw him out of the communal bed! Oh, my God!' He slammed his fist into his palm. 'I admit, if I was around when it happened, I'd kill him! I would wreak bloody havoc! I am your serpent and I don't belong. So I'm leaving. But there's no bloody chance that I'm leaving you behind. Now come on!'

Hugo's fury had made him reckless, he had no thought for the brutes around him. He grabbed her arm and she pulled back.

'No, Hugo, leave me here! Go away!'

His rage increased and he slapped her face, half intending, God help him, to knock her out and take her by force. She screamed and he lifted her bodily, struggling in his arms, and began to carry her towards the forest through the ranks of naked figures still lying motionless on the grass.

They all stood up at the same instant – as they had done before – as if by an unseen signal.

Hugo paused for a second, looking at the closed ranks facing him, then roared his contempt.

'Out of my way, you helpless bloody freaks. No more messages of brotherly love, just let me get back to the devil I know. And for Christ's sake, don't sing "Aloha" on the

178

way out! Now move!'

The mutants made no attempt to move. Nor did they sing 'Aloha'. Nor was the music, when it came, the sweet ethereal sound. It was a threnody of despair, reviving the traces of some primordial memory, telling more of suffering and pity than all the elegies and requiems of the Masters.

Hugo found himself unable to move. The vibrations were probing and dragging at the walls of his stomach, he was actually feeling the nausea of grief and heartbreak. He was unable to hold Jenny, he had to release his grip and let her fall to the grass. The music was changing, rising to a higher pitch like an escape of scalding steam and the pain was moving upwards, up into his chest, crushing his lungs – he couldn't breathe – up, up to his head, into his brain. An unbearable pressure was building up inside his skull, pulsating, swelling into a throbbing, blinding spasm until, all at once, he was screaming in agony! But the scream was soaked up in the grim harmony of the voices, he was joining them in their song of death.

They were killing him! Killing him with sonic vibrations, destroying the serpent in their midst with the music of The Garden!

As he felt his consciousness slipping away, knew he could do nothing to save himself, he was only vaguely aware that Jenny had risen to her feet, tears streaming down her face, that she was holding him in her arms, struggling vainly to keep him from sinking to his knees.

'Huggy, Huggy, my love! Oh, please!' She turned her face to the Neanders. 'Please – don't . . . hurt . . . him!'

The harmonies fluttered for the barest moment.

'He isn't trying to harm me!'

The music stopped. Then, as if transposed into a new mode of mercy and forgiveness, it opened up again with all its old, celestial grandeur, its message of love. Hugo's 'helpless, bloody freaks' were sparing his life, responding

179

to Jenny's plea.

Hugo stayed crouching there for a moment, staring down at the blades of green grass in front of him. There was no pain. No trace of the relentless vice that had been crushing him. No anger, no hatred. Only a feeling of peace and calm.

Jenny was kneeling at his side, still holding him tenderly in her arms.

'My love, my darling old Hugo.' He looked up at her and smiled, then lowered his head, encased in its silly plastic mask, on to her shoulder. 'They didn't want to hurt you. They were protecting me. Then they saw what you never could – that I have always loved you more than anyone else in the world. But you have always doubted me. The only difference now is that I love all these people as much as you. And none of them doubts me. Now do you see, my love, now do you understand? To love one person above all others is the fatal flaw, the Human Tragedy. In such a love, there must always be pain.'

Hugo lifted his head slowly and looked at her. He looked at her for a long time. Then he closed his eyes and let his mind go blank.

Chapter Sixteen

Kurnitz and Linda were waiting for them at the tunnel linking The Garden to The Ark. They said nothing as Hugo and Jenny appeared from the forest, but turned and led the way to the air-lock.

When they reached it, Hugo held Jenny for a moment, with no awareness of parting, no sense of finality in their look at each other. Then he was through the air-lock, with Kurnitz and Linda, they were going through decontamination procedures, under the shower, removing the suits, washing hands and face, final check by automatic monitor, still with no word passing between them.

Not until Linda was opening the door to Control Room 'B' did Kurnitz speak or show any sign of emotion. Then he said: 'Go ahead, Linda, pacify them but don't say what has happened. I want a chat with Dr Brill. Thank you.'

Kurnitz sat down in the small ante-chamber and sighed heavily. Hugo made no attempt to look at him, no attempt to speak.

'Well, Dr Brill,' he said at last, 'I am incapable of making you an adequate apology and I owe you a debt of gratitude which I do not think I can ever repay. I think you know what I mean.'

Hugo would not look at him. He was not sure whether he felt more contempt for the old man's ruthlessness than admiration for his genius.

'I knew you were leading us somewhere, Kurnitz, but I read the signs wrongly. I thought the arrows all pointed to Jenny. Then I suspected that the human guinea-pig was going to be me. But I didn't realise that the subjects under test were your own children.'

'I had to find out,' Kurnitz was actually embarrassed, 'how my children would react to danger. I had to know how they would apply their intellect and ingenuity to an alien threat. Your wife was no use to me. Ha! The first human being to be let into The Garden and she was one of their own kind. But then, of course, she was a threat to Fallon, she was let into The Garden *because* she was one of them. Ironic! However. Then you appeared on the scene and the temptation was too great.'

'So you let me in. Let me remove the suit, the alien mask – knowing that I was a full-blooded serpent who sooner or later was going to wreak havoc because he didn't trust his wife.'

Kurnitz sighed again and shook his head. 'I would prefer to say too much in love with his wife.' He looked at Hugo keenly. 'But I promise you, when I let you in I had no idea what their reaction would be. If any. In their innocence they may have had no resource. They could have let you ride rough-shod over them and given in. In which case, their chances of survival outside would have been nil.' He lifted his hands into the air, his eyes wide with surprise. 'The music! The innocuous, charming music is their strength – their defence, their attack. Enormous resonant cavities, of course! Ha! My Saints have sharp teeth, the

182

power to destroy.' He lowered his hands to his knees and smiled. 'But only to protect their own. They will use their power wisely, with compassion. With such an armoury, my children are going to survive, thank God.' Hugo said nothing, still looked away. Kurnitz shifted in his chair. 'You must believe, Dr Brill, that I had no knowledge of this power. I would never have exposed you to such danger –'

'Please, Kurnitz! Spare me that! I think you would, but the point is academic. What about Jenny?'

'Ach!' Kurnitz stood up and paced for a moment. 'She belongs in there. The choice to stay or go has always been hers. But she will be safe. And I think you now know that her happiness will be guaranteed.' The old man was restless, ill at ease. 'So! What will you do, Dr Brill? Leave her there or raise hell to get her out before Stage Two?' Hugo said nothing. 'Fallon will want to keep you under guard, at least until the time is up.' Hugo was silent. 'He may want to keep you in custody indefinitely – another heartless cover-up – because you could promise to be silent, then go outside and – pouf! I would beg you to keep my secret, but I can ask no more of you. I am already too deeply in your debt. I am truly sorry for all the pain I have caused you ... I will do all I can to make amends.' He looked at the silent Hugo for a few seconds, then opened the door to Control Room 'B'. 'We may as well go in,' he said.

Chapter Seventeen

Fallon was waiting for them, bristling with anger.
'I don't know what the hell has been going on in
there! But I do know the bloody girl didn't give in!' He
thumped his fist into his hand over and over. 'Well, let her
rot in there, the stubborn –'

'Shut up!' said Hugo.

'Dr Brill, you do not appreciate the seriousness of your
own position! I must warn –'

'I said shut up!'

Hugo walked across to Fallon, took him carefully by the
lapels and stared directly into his eyes.

'You are a serpent, and you speak with forked tongue!
Furthermore, you are not fit to be associated with one
microcosmic particle of the miracle that has been happening
inside those walls! But that is because you happen to be a
particularly definitive specimen of a licensed executioner
who is only doing his job!' He let go Fallon's lapels and
noticed, with some satisfaction, that Rogers was making no
attempt to interfere. 'Well, Major, I have news for you.

Your job is done! My wife, God bless her, is staying in there, and even if she wasn't she would keep your lousy secret. Because she, like me, would be going out there into the big, wide world, determined never to breathe to a living soul one word of the wonders that we have experienced! You certainly will not comprehend or believe this, and I don't give a damn if you do or not!'

Fallon glowered at him. 'I cannot take the responsibility for letting you out, because I don't believe you are willing to leave your wife inside that –'

'I will take the responsibility!'

Hugo looked round. Kurnitz was studying him with an unusual look. It was a mixture of warm affection, appraisal – and something else.

'I will take full responsibility for Dr Brill, because, as I had dared to hope, he understands.' Kurnitz crossed to Hugo and took his hand tightly in both of his own. 'You are a brave man, my friend! And a selfless one. You will have a permanent written authority to visit The Garden whenever you wish.' He looked over towards Barnes, who nodded at once. 'You can, of course, visit your wife as often as you like. We want you to keep in touch. And one day, who knows –'

'When I am ready?'

'When you are ready,' nodded Kurnitz.

'In a state of grace,' murmured Hugo quietly. He shook hands with Linda Benson, who, quite unexpectedly, gave him a warm hug. Now at last he was able to trust the light in her eyes, the evangelical zeal.

'I'll see you to your car,' said Barnes. 'Will you be driving back to London this evening?'

'No,' said Hugo, 'I'll stay the night at the Cold Pike Hotel. I'd like to be nearby for a little longer.' He shook his head, fighting back a sudden wave of emotion. 'Probably go back tomorrow.'

185

As they reached the door, Hugo turned back.

'Oh, Dr Kurnitz, I think I have a name for your new species.'

'What's that, my friend?'

'Homo Benedictus,' said Hugo, then his eyes flicked for an instant to Fallon. 'Kind man.'

Barnes said very little as he escorted Hugo back through the Centre, up in the lift, and out to his car. It was a strange feeling to be outside again, to find that it was still daylight.

Barnes shook him warmly by the hand.

'I needn't tell you how much you have done for us. As for Fallon,' he shook his head, 'I have no doubt that he will be transferred to duties more to his liking very soon.'

Hugo had a brief picture of the Major back in the field, with refurbished cloak and dagger, sniffing out 'moles' in Whitehall or opium dealers in Hong Kong. Still doing his job.

As he drove back along the winding lanes towards the hotel, he wondered why he had no feeling of loss, no onset of the bitter grief that he had been dreading for the last two days. He let his mind slowly open up again, allowed himself to think of Jenny, back there in that bizarre tropical Garden, tucked away somewhere underground in a tiny corner of the Cumbrian coast. He switched on the radio, tuned in some music, and resolutely kept his eyes on the road, never looking back.

He was soon passing Gosforth, aware of the trees and the flowers and the sky and the red sandstone buildings, listening to the birdsong filling the air around him, thinking of Regent's Park and Clare Market and the White Pond at Hampstead, musing on the 'beauty, horror and immensity' of nature that would open up before him tomorrow on the way back to London.

Could Jenny give all this up? Give him up too, so easily? Never to hold each other close again? Blast the music, it

186

was too sentimental! He pressed the tuning button.

'*News Headlines. John Beecher, a machine operator, has been suspended for three months for working too hard. Last week, he was sent to Coventry by his fellow workers, incensed by the amount he earns in piece-work. The management regard him as a trouble-maker.*'

He was passing a picturesque little restaurant, nestling behind a trimmed hedge on the side of the road, and thought about the very special meals he had shared with Jenny in so many special places . . . paté and asparagus and Chablis and Chateaubriand and Medoc and mange-tout and paillard de veau; fish and chips and a cup of tea; smoked Irish salmon and a creamy draught Guinness; candy floss and an ice-cream on the pier; a Havana cigar and a glass of Cointreau; a foaming pint on a hot summer's day; the joys of living, the joys of life. . . .

'*West German police have allowed three of their most wanted terrorists to slip through their fingers; now security experts fear the notorious Baader-Meinhof gang may be planning a new series of terror attacks.*'

The joys of living, the joys of life . . . Montmartre in the spring, the cobbled road winding up the hill to the first view of the Sacre-Coeur; strolling around Fisherman's Wharf in San Francisco and Farmer's Market on Fairfax in Los Angeles; anywhere in Rome, Jenny's Rome, the Eternal City. . . .

'*Ten passengers who survived a Rhodesian airliner crash twelve miles south of Lake Kariba were lined up and massacred by black nationalist guerillas of the Zipra army.*'

He was looking up at the clear sky and the sun moving westwards to wind up the day, driving once more toward the joys of living, driving away from the dearest thing in his life, leaving Jenny behind and beyond his reach. And still no sense of loss, no grief, no pain. He sighed deeply and frowned. It was puzzling. No pain . . . onward, Hugo

187

. . . toward the joys of life . . . in a wide world of wonder and beauty. . . .

'*A widow of seventy was tortured by a gang of boys and girls aged between twelve and thirteen to make her hand over her weekly pension. They broke her fingers, kicked her kneecaps, twisted her arms, cut her hair, and forced her to drink urine, in an ordeal that lasted eight months. The case only came to light when the local council sued her for £100 in rent arrears.*'

Hugo switched off the radio. Jenny had given all this up. Was that why he felt no pain? Knowing she was safe from the callous, black terrors, forever swirling round the joys of life like thick globs of pollution in a spring of clear water? Knowing where she was, knowing he could see her whenever he wanted? Was this why he felt no pain? Or was it something more? Much more than that?

'To love one person above all others is the fatal flaw, the Human Tragedy. In such a love, there must always be pain.'

Jenny's words had silenced him in The Garden, turned in his mind, like a key unlocking a secret door. Now he was finding what lay on the other side. Eternal passion, eternal pain! Must the passion be for mankind, must the love for one's neighbour be as rich and full as the love for one's mate? And if such a pure, limitless, universal love, given without suspicion and fear and distrust, was the love that Hugo had never found, could it only exist inside The Garden? Or was it to be found out here, in a world where beauty and horror went side by side?

Jenny had had it all the time. He had not. All those years he had insulted her with feelings unworthy of her love for him. So she had searched for something beyond him, found it at last in The Garden, behind the secret door, where her own species, Homo Benedictus, had been waiting for her to come home. He had lost her to them, yet still he had no feeling of loss; because at last he understood the quality of her love. In losing her, he had come to terms with himself.

188

'And the joke of it is, Hugo,' he said to himself, with a wry, wry smile. 'The joke is that now, at last, you feel no pain! Which would suggest, my clever friend, to recoin a phrase, that you have loved, not too wisely, but too bloody late!'

He parked outside the Cold Pike Hotel and went in. His old room was still vacant and he booked it, wasn't sure if he could face it sober, so he left his bags with the ever-smiling receptionist and went into the bar.

Miss Sweden was back, and asked after his wife. He told her Jenny was still around, working hard, they'd been in touch and would meet back in London in a couple of days.

Blast you, Fallon, he said to himself, now you've got me doing your dirty work!

It was dusk by the time he had drunk himself into a euphoria that would protect him from a lapse of faith. Well, it was early days yet! But as he went up the stairs to dear old Cell 27, the dread of the loneliness ahead, beginning with this empty room, was growing in him. He fumbled the key in the lock for a few seconds before he realised the door was open. The light was on! He peered in and saw to his embarrassment that the bed was occupied.

'I'm most terribly sorry, I must have the wrong –'

At that moment, as if in a flash of blinding light, he recalled Kurnitz's face, the unusual look in the old man's eyes that had puzzled Hugo as he was leaving the control room. Now he knew what it was! It was a look of decision! Kurnitz, in his infinite wisdom, born of a long heritage of suffering and pain and compassion, had made his own decision about the nature of love and the quality of mercy that lies within it.

Chapter Eighteen

'Come in, Huggy,' said Jenny.

He came in. And dropped his suitcase on the floor.

'Mr Barnes brought me over. They said you were in the bar, so I thought it might be a nice surprise if I waited for you here.'

Hugo's coat was joining the suitcase on the floor.

'Abba, you see,' she continued, wriggling up on the pillow, 'has a theory. He postulates that once in a hundred lifetimes, there comes along a love so very special that it cannot be divided between separate worlds. To do so would create a tension within each world and that is something he would not care to risk.'

Hugo's tie was somewhere on the washstand, his shirt was racing from his shoulders towards the armchair.

'Now, I think that dear old Abba is a tiny bit equivocal, not to say devious, when it suits him, but I didn't find myself arguing too much. Especially since I'd arrived at the same conclusion – in a different way of course. You see, I've been thinking. Abba and Linda and Jessie Barratt –

190

and, of course, myself – all live outside The Garden. But as John said, we are all, without any spontaneous mutation, ready to go in. Oh, that reminds me, Linda told me that Abba has decided to let Jessie join her husband. Isn't that nice? Where was I, oh yes, and as you yourself said so brilliantly, there must be more like us outside.'

Hugo was pulling at the lace on his shoe, tying it into an inextricable knot, cursing quietly under his breath.

'So what I want to do is find them and start a kind of Garden of our own, out *here*! Our watchword would be: *Homo Benedictus* – Abba told me that was your idea and I like it – *Homo Benedictus is already amongst us*! Why don't you pull the bloody shoe off!'

Hugo ripped off his shoe, then the other, and started on the trousers.

'Meanwhile, Abba wants us to keep in touch and he'll make tests on us periodically to see we're alright. Oh yes, and he said I can come back into The Garden for good, only when you are ready. Which, of course, is very unlikely, though I'm ready already, my love, but then you never did really understand me, did you? Well, actually I'm ready but still a bit old-fashioned like you. About sex, I mean. And I haven't quite used you up yet, so I don't really need anybody else for the rest of my life, do I?'

Hugo was climbing into bed, as naked as Plum and far less impressive. None of which seemed to concern Jenny at all.

'I know I was inside longer than you, Huggy, but they decontaminated me quite thoroughly, there's no need to keep your distance.'

After a very long moment, Hugo stopped kissing her, lifted his head and looked into her eyes.

'Well, I have news for you, beloved child.' He reached for the light switch. '*I'm ready!*'

191